BODIE BEAUTIES

"Bastard! You shot me!" the gunman said.

"My calling card," McCoy said from where he hid behind his boulder. "Who hired you? Was it the men who held up the stage and killed the guards?"

"Don't know what you're talking about. Jesus, I'm bleeding to death."

"Tell me who hired you and I'll take you down to Doc Rogers."

"Not if I kill you first."

"You tried and missed. Now it's my turn!"

Also in the *Spur* Series:

SPUR #26

BODIE BEAUTIES

DIRK FLETCHER

LEISURE BOOKS NEW YORK CITY

A LEISURE BOOK®

July 2005

Published by

Dorchester Publishing Co., Inc.
200 Madison Avenue
New York, NY 10016

ISBN 0-8439-2635-X

Visit us on the web at www.dorchesterpub.com.

BODIE
BEAUTIES

1

Wesley Urick saw the shadowy figures in the trees and knew instinctively that they had trouble. He drew his six-gun and blasted a shot into the cool California night air rousing the six armed men inside the Concord stagecoach that jolted along a high mountain trail from the booming mining town of Bodie toward Bridgeport.

"Trouble!" Wesley shouted, bringing up the double barreled Greener.

A rifle snarled in the woods, a heavy sound like a big Sharps-Borchardt, Wesley thought. A fraction of a second later the .45-70 round from the rifle slammed into his chest, tore through his heart and out his back, taking a two-inch chunk of his spinal column with it.

The dead body that seconds before had been Wesley jolted off the high seat of the Concord, pitched to the side and smashed into the ground as the stagecoach rumbled on past.

By then a dozen guns had barked from the woods on both sides of the coach. The attackers had picked the perfect spot, the man with the reins directing the four horses knew. At this point they were at the steepest up slope on the route and he had been forced to slow to a walk to negotiate the hill and the rutted stage road.

From inside the coach, six well armed men began returning fire. All had rifles and pistols, but there were few chances to see the attackers.

A high pitched scream stabbed through the darkness and the coach stopped abruptly.

"Bastards shot a lead horse!" one of the six guards inside the coach shouted over the gunfire. "Make your shots count. Whoever is out there knows what they're doing."

"Goddamn, I'm hit!" one of the guards inside the crowded coach shouted. Then he pitched forward against another guard who had his Spencer repeating rifle aimed out the window, the other guard dead before he fell. He saw a rider in the darkness of the woods and fired. There was a moment of satisfaction as he saw him blasted off the horse.

But ten seconds later six rounds came through the open curtain where the guard with the Spencer sat. Two of the hot chunks of lead bored into his skull stripping all life from his suddenly limp body.

Another Wells Fargo Stage Lines guard, Frank Gaston, crowded lower in the Concord. He sat on the floor, his Remington repeater angled over the low door. Both the shotgun guard and the driver had to be dead. They would go in the first volley. Now two more inside had died.

"Ain't worth it!" Frank shouted. "Let's give the bastards the gold." He went on in a much calmer tone as the three other men inside stopped firing.

"Hell, I ain't gonna die for somebody else's gold. Not for three dollars a day, I ain't."

The other three guards agreed.

"Stop shooting!" Frank called out. "Enough! Dammit, we give up! You done killed half of us now. Ease off and you can have the fucking gold!"

The men firing weapons on both sides of the coach slowed their shooting and then stopped. A voice came out of the blackness. "How many alive inside?" a heavy voice asked.

"Four. Only four."

"Throw out your weapons, rifles and six-guns," the voice snarled.

The guards threw out eight rifles and six pistols.

"That everything?"

"Damn right!" Frank bellowed.

Somebody in the darkness laughed.

"Get out one at a time and lace your fingers in back of your necks. Now!"

The four guards did as they were told.

The clouds slid away from the moon and brightened the scene. The driver lay sprawled just behind the coach. Frank couldn't see the shotgun guard.

Men on horses still shrouded in the darkness, moved up slowly.

"Well now. Look a' here. You gents ain't Pinkertons, know for damn sure. Just local hires pretending to be guards."

A robber rode in on the other side of the stagecoach and stepped up to the driver's seat where he opened the front boot.

"Got it!" the man shouted. "Strong box is up here and it's heavy as hell!"

"Get it out of there," the leader in the darkness ordered.

The coach rattled as two men tugged the strong

box out of the boot and tossed it to the ground.

Saddle leather creaked as men dismounted. One moved into the soft moonlight in front of the four prisoners. He turned quickly as someone shouted. The kerchief that had been hiding his face came loose and fell around his neck.

He looked up at the four men, pawing at the cloth to cover his face.

"Lenny! You bastard!" Frank shouted. "What the hell you doing here? You're Lenny and I use to play poker with you at the Richstrike Saloon!" Too late, Frank realized what he'd done.

"Oh, damn, Lenny, I promise I won't ever breathe a word. Give me a horse and I'll be in Oregon in a week and claim I never been in California. Won't tell a soul, Lenny, I promise!"

Lenny drew his six-gun and leveled it at Frank. "Shit, Frank, didn't know you was gonna be on this run. How'n hell was I to know? Not a damn thing I can do now, Frank. If'n it was just me, you could ride. But, hell, you know these other gents won't hear of that."

A shot blasted into the stillness on the other side of the coach.

"Get that strong box open?" Lenny asked.

"Damn right, come look!" a voice beyond the rig shouted.

"Bring the whole box around here and don't open it," Lenny snapped.

"Lenny, you can't do this," Frank pleaded. "Look, there's four human beings here. You can't just execute us, shoot us down in cold blood. You just can't do that. They can't be paying you enough. . . ."

Lenny shot Frank Gaston in the chest, then once

more in the side of the head as he fell. The sound of the first shot sent the other three guards on the Wells Fargo stage into action. They charged away into the darkness in three different directions.

Lenny shot the closest one through the back of the head, sent two bullets at the next one but missed. Three more pistols and a rifle roared in the mountain air, and the other two guards fell in the moonlight along the deserted mountain stagecoach trail.

"Make sure of them," Lenny said.

A few minutes later, he heard a pistol blast once, then twice.

"Damn sure of all four of them now," a voice said in the blackness.

When the two men lugged the heavy strong box around the stage, Lenny found some dry grass and twisted up a torch, then lit it with a stinker match and lifted the lid.

Inside lay fifteen gold bars, each weighing five pounds.

"Don't any of you get any wild ideas or even think about taking off on your own," Lenny said. "California ain't big enough for you to hide. Your skin would be worth five-thousand dollars to me if you try it."

He picked up the bars, hefted them. "Yeah, worth more money than we ever saw before, but it ain't ours. I saw Les get knocked off his mount. He hit hard?"

"He's dead," a voice answered.

"Damn, he was good. Two of you drag him back off the trail and pile some brush over him. Somebody else bring his horse around."

When the holdup men got back from hiding the body, Lenny had the gold bars split between his own saddle bags and those of the horse Les had ridden. He tried a lead line on the nag and then Lenny studied the immediate site.

A few minutes later he began giving orders. One man cut the dead horse out of the leather harness, and using his horse, dragged the carcass to the edge of a small canyon, twenty feet from the trail, and rolled the stiffening animal down the fifty foot dropoff.

They drove the stage to the same place, shot the three horses, and toppled the stage over the bank, dragging the horses with it.

It took them longer to find the dead guards but when they did, their bodies also were dumped into the open grave of the canyon. When they were done, no trace remained of the stage.

"Let's ride," Lenny said. "When we get back to town you'll all get paid. Anybody who wants to ride out, should head for Nevada. For the money you made tonight, you can afford a small vacation."

Lenny kept the other five men ahead of him as they rode along the trail toward Bodie. They had hit the gold stage about fifteen miles from the mining town, and now went back over the easy trail at a canter, eating up almost six miles an hour. It was still dark when they came to the outskirts of a sleeping town that showed lights around the gold and silver mines and stamping mills and in some of the saloons along Main Street.

Lenny pulled his men to a stop just outside of town and dug into his pocket.

"Like I told you before, you each get a hundred dollars. That's more real money than you've seen in a long time. Don't spent it all in one day in Bodie or Captain Trevarow will have you in jail before you can spit. He's old, but he's smart. Better if you ride out to Auroa or Hawthorne where it won't matter if you whoop it up a little."

"Figured since we done such a good job, we'd get a few dollars more," a whining voice said from one of the men in the darkness.

Lenny eased his six-gun from leather. "You get $100 or you get three cents worth of lead. Which you want?"

Lenny paid the last man. He sat his horse and rolled a smoke while he watched them ride away. Two of them said they would stay in town. The other three chose to keep riding right on through toward Nevada. Lenny was pleased, there would be three fewer witnesses to worry about.

He caught the lead line to the second horse and angled around the main part of town to the west. He climbed the hill behind the town where the mines dotted the landscape. A quarter of a mile beyond the Standard Stamp Mill, he came to a mine works and tied the horses to an office hitching rail.

A cigar glowed in the darkness of the porch.

"Figured that was you, Lenny," the voice said.

Lenny jumped, then grinned. "Yeah, and right on time. Got something for you."

"All of it?"

"Seventy-five pounds worth."

"Let's take it around back," the same even voice said.

"Ran into some trouble. Lost one man. Somebody recognized me so we had to make sure nobody talked."

"All eight of them?"

"Yes."

"Christ, gonna be hell to pay."

13

"Just couldn't be helped."

They stopped at the back door of a long low shed, lifted the saddle bags off and carried them inside.

Two coal oil lamps burned brightly. The room was next door to the area where raw gold was melted down and poured into molds with the mine's name stamped proudly into the top of each bar for all to see.

The tall man with handlebar moustache and long sideburns took the gold bars from the saddle bags and stacked them on the table.

"Fifteen, right. You say you lost a man?"

"Yeah, Les. Shot through the heart."

"Tough. You can have his pay."

"Thanks, I earned it. You offered me a thousand besides if I brought back the gold."

"That, plus a bonus."

The tall man's voice had a faint note of sarcasm and Lenny looked up. The grin on his face changed to a scowl and then the start of a scream as the .45 the tall man held fired and the heavy round smashed into Lenny's open mouth, traveled upward through the roof of his mouth and into his brain where it tore up a dozen vital nerve centers before it shattered into ten fragments which lodged against his thick skull bone.

The tall man called softly. "Newman. You have a job to do."

The man who came through a side door was about forty, stooped, with a reddish complexion from too much sun, too much foundry heat, or too much whiskey. He had a crooked face, damaged by a mule that had kicked him when he was a boy. His cheek had been caved in and never repaired. The flesh under one eye was torn and still sagged to the side, and his mouth was ripped and healed with a large scar and pulled down to one side and usually dripped with a disgusting drool.

Newman nodded, didn't seem surprised to see the dead man. He simply picked up Lenny's body and dragged it out the door. He slung it over the saddle of one of the horses and tied it on securely. He would dump it well out of town where it might not be found for months.

Before he moved the horse, he went back into the workroom and mopped up the blood, then waved to his benefactor and hurried out to dispose of the body.

The tall man wearing a black suit preened his moustache and hefted the bars. He frowned at the name on the top of each one: STD-BODIE. They were from the Standard Mining Company there in Bodie. That would be changed soon enough. He moved quickly through the mostly dark headquarters building of the mine until he came to a door where he knocked. He could see light under the panel.

A voice answered and he opened the door a foot and talked around it.

"Everything is going according to plan. We have the seventy-five pounds of bars and will get to work on them shortly. By morning they will be completely safe."

"Good. Give me a report in the morning."

The tall man said he would, closed the door and hurried back to the foundry room. He had come up through mining, knew every phase of the operation. That's why he made such a good manager of this mine.

Now he took off his suit coat and vest and built up

the fire. Then one by one he put the gold bars in the heavy iron cauldron where they would melt.

As they did he added a like number of gold bars already cast with their own imprint on them. When the gold was melted and mingled, no chemist on earth could tie it down as coming from any particular seam or vein of raw gold ore—so not from any one mine.

Also with their own imprint on the bars, they could send them to the mint in San Francisco and not an eyelash would be raised.

The man worked quickly, efficiently, and when Newman returned, the disfigured little man helped do the pouring for the new bullion bars. Newman was an expert at his trade and the tall man welcomed his help even though it was hard to look at the ugly face.

When they completed the pouring and the molds were cooling, Newman gave his superior the money he found on Lenny's body, more than three hundred dollars.

"Thank you, Newman, that will be all. And remember, not a word of this to anyone, or I'll cut your balls off so you'll never again be able to go see Miss Lily's girls up in Virgin Alley, you understand?"

"Yes . . . yes sir. I don't talk. Never have."

Newman stood watching the tall man for a moment, then hurried out the door to his small shack on the mine grounds where the mine owner said that he could live.

After preening his handlebar moustache again, the tall man smiled. They had just cleared $74,700 for the company, and he was determined to have his ten percent of that. The mine owner had promised him that—and he would collect.

2

The Wells Fargo stage came toward Bodie from the south along the regular stage road from Bridgeport. Spur McCoy stretched in the close confines of the coach and then stared out the window at the booming mining town on the far fringes of California next to Nevada.

It had been a tiring stage ride from the end of the railroad at Sacramento, and Spur was happy to see the town. It was laid out north and south along Main Street on a flat that was nearly two miles long and about half a mile wide. The back side of the town, now home to from ten thousand to thirteen thousand souls, sloped up into the low ridges that had provided the reason all these people were here— gold and silver ore.

More than a dozen smoke stacks belched smoke where wood furnaces provided steam for the mine works and the stamping mills. Even from a mile away he could hear the clanging of metal on metal as the stamping mills turned rocky gold ore into a finer consistency that could be worked.

Spur McCoy leaned on the window watching the town come into closer view. He was a tall man, two-inches over six-feet, and a rugged two-hundred pounds. He wore his reddish brown hair a little long around the ears, but that was because he seldom found time to sit for a barber. His full moustache met sandy muttonchop sideburns but his chin and neck were shaven clean.

Curious green eyes stared out at the world and his tanned and windburned face showed that he spent as many hours in the weather and under the stars at night as he did indoors.

A drummer sitting beside Spur looked at the town and chuckled. "Don't look so rough to me," the drummer said. "Heard about a little girl who was moving here with her parents and she said, 'Good-bye God, we're moving to Bodie!' "

Spur laughed and began checking the buildings on the outskirts of town. The cemetery showed to the left on the first slope up from the flatland. Down lower he saw a sign on a wood frame building that proclaimed it was Moyle Storage.

To the right of Main Street he saw three or four houses and a larger building that looked like a church. Close by Main stood the Moyle Bottling Works. This place had grown ten times the size it was the last time Spur had hurried through five years ago. Gold did strange things to a town.

Spur McCoy came to Bodie to look up an old friend. Spur was a Secret Service Agent of the United States government. The service had been established by Congress in 1865 specifically to protect the currency from counterfeiting. Since then it had taken on the police duties of any matter that crossed from one state line or territory into another.

Spur had joined the agency shortly after it began and was a crack shot with pistol, rifle, shotgun, derringer, and an excellent horseman. He was in great physical condition and an expert at hand-to-hand fighting with fists, knife or staff. He was unabashedly a ladies' man and they couldn't keep their hands off him. They found his rugged good looks, his Harvard education, soft spoken manner and his gentleness so unlike most of the Western men they knew.

Spur's father was a well known New York merchant. After graduating from Harvard University in Boston, Spur had worked in his father's firms for a while. Then he went into the army as a Lieutenant and served the Union army for two years before going to Washington, D.C. to be an aide to an old family friend who was a U.S. Senator from New York.

After he joined the Secret Service, he was soon appointed to head up the Western region of the agency with headquarters in St. Louis. He had as his area all those states and territories west of the Mississippi River.

The big Concord stage jolted over some ruts, then rolled into the canyon of Bodie's main street with stores and offices and shops along both sides for a good half mile.

Bodie was wood. Spur could see no stone or brick buildings as he rode down Main to the Wells Fargo stage office across from the Occidental Hotel. Spur had heard tall tales about the bad men of Bodie, now he probably would see a few of them in action. He had come to town from Sacramento to visit an old friend, Sheriff's Captain John Trevarow.

The county seat had been in Bridgeport since

1864, Spur knew, so that's where the County Sheriff was. John said he had been appointed Chief Deputy for Bodie, had been given twenty deputies, and the rank of Captain. His letter had been concise.

"McCoy, I'm getting slow and won't admit it except to you. It's the damn rheumatiz in my right hand. I can still shoot good as ever, but it's the draw. I look like my Aunt Matilda drawing out of leather.

"Not too sure that I can hold my temper if one of the young punks around here wants to make a name for himself and call me out. Had one or two want to try, but I joshed them out of it.

"It would be dandy if you could pay me a visit next time you're out this way and maybe discourage some of the local riff-raff who think they're fast but ain't never seen a real fast draw."

The letter was dated two months ago and caught up with Spur in Denver. He hoped the old lawman was still alive.

Spur swung down from the stage at the depot, caught his carpet bag from the top and stashed it at the U.S. Hotel, the best in town and across Wood Street from the Occidental. His room cost a dollar a night. He paid for three days in advance, then went to talk to Sheriff's Captain Trevarow.

The Bodie jail sat on the corner of Bonanza and King Streets, north of the hotel and a block west of Main. Captain Trevarow's office was there as well. A deputy at a small desk just inside the door pointed west.

"Captain and two men just went up to Virgin Alley," the young deputy said. "Peers a customer of one of the ladies of the evening had some trouble."

Spur thanked the deputy and walked along King Street to where it began climbing the upgrade to the

Bodie houses of ill repute which perched there on the side of the hill. They had been neatly segregated from the "proper" citizens so none of the "nice" ladies would be contaminated.

He found Virgin Alley next to Maiden Lane and Virtue Street, with thirty or forty men and demimondes gathered around some kind of a confrontation outside the fancy Highgrade brothel.

Spur worked his way through the shirtsleeve crowd. Even though it was August, at 8,500 feet there's always a little bite in the air and the ever present Bodie wind blowing that varied from light to sturdy.

When Spur got to the center of things he saw a barefoot man in his undershirt and pants waving a six-inch hunting knife at two sheriff's deputies. Both had on badges but that didn't deter the knife man.

"I wanta fight the sheriff!" the man yelled. Spur could see blood on the edge of the blade the man held. A second man lay near his feet with a six-inch gash on his upper arm that he tried to hold together with one hand to slow the bleeding.

"Where's the goddamned Sheriff?" the knifer bellowed.

"I'm the best we've got for a sheriff," a tall, slender man who looked to be about sixty said and stepped forward. "County Sheriff is over at Bridgeport. You new in town?"

"Want to kill me a sheriff," the man said. Now it was obvious to Spur that the knife wielder was drunk, almost too plastered to stand up. He transferred the bloody knife to his left hand and let his right hang beside a six-gun holstered on his hip.

"You're packing a piece, Sheriff, you draw first," the drunk thundered.

"No cause for this, mister. You just put down the knife and come down to the jail and sleep it off. Then you'll be back to work tomorrow."

"Want to shoot me a fucking Sheriff!" the drunk screamed.

The people watching all edged back. Those behind Captain Trevarow and the drunk hurried to one side to get out of the line of any possible shooting.

"The Sheriff is over in Bridgeport. I'm Captain Trevarow, head of the sheriff's office here. Why don't we talk this over. You got drunk and you cut up that man. He needs to get over to Doc Rogers before he loses that arm. You come along now peaceful like and we'll only charge you for stitching up the arm. Fair enough?"

The drunk drew his six-gun. He was better than most, but still not very fast, Spur decided. The drunk put the weapon back in his holster and looked up, blinking away some film over his eyes.

"Damnit, want to kill me a Sheriff!"

Spur eased up beside Trevarow and glared at the drunk. His .45 Colt was tied low on his right leg in its usual place. The well oiled weapon was loaded and ready. The leather was polished with neatsfoot oil and supple.

"Mister, you just pretend I'm the Sheriff, all right?" Spur said evenly. "Now look over there at that weathervane on top of the house. You see it?"

The drunk scowled for a minute, turned and nearly fell, stared at the house, then nodded. "Yeah, see it. So what?"

"Watch," Spur said.

Some people said they never saw his hand move. In the blink of an eyelash Spur drew the Colt, thumbed back the hammer and fired from the hip. The roar of the six-gun going off startled the crowd.

The "W" on the weathervane caught the .45 slug, gave off a clang and the weathervane spun around a dozen times from the impact.

The men in the group stared in surprise. It was a four-inch square target at more than eighty feet.

"Christ' a'mighty! You see that shot?" one of the men shouted.

"Talk about fast! That was so damn fast I barely saw his hand move!" someone else added.

Spur holstered the weapon, moved his feet to a slightly wider stance and looked back at the drunk.

"Now, let's just pretend that I'm that Sheriff you want to kill. You go ahead and draw against me, just anytime you're ready."

The drunk's eyes were still wide in wonder.

"You . . . you really did that? He hit the weathervane?" The drunk looked around at the others.

They nodded.

"Damn right he did," a fancy lady wearing a petticoat and little else said.

"Yeah, he did. You wanta be dead, crazy man, you just go ahead and try to outdraw him," another voice said.

The drunk turned back to Spur. He pushed the bloody knife into a sheath and stared again at the tall man a dozen feet from him.

"Are . . . are you somebody? A fast gun or something?"

"What do you care? You want to draw against a Sheriff. Go ahead." The deadly, cold tone of Spur's voice shocked the drunk back another step. He hit a rock in the street, stumbled and fell.

The two deputies helped him stand up. He shook off their hands.

"What's your name?" Spur demanded in a tone that brought a sure response.

"Wanamaker, W. W. Wanamaker. Why?" the drunk asked.

"Sometimes they don't know what name to put on a grave marker," Spur said softly. His hand moved slightly next to his holster, fingers relaxed, ready.

Slowly the drunk held up his hands. He shook his head. "No offense, mister. I think I'll go with the Captain there, have a nice sleep in his jail."

The deputies lifted the pistol and knife from Wanamaker's belt, caught both his arms and walked him down the slope toward King Street and the Bodie jail.

The crowd slowly dispersed, the excitement over. Some of the soiled doves tarried, watching the tall stranger who had backed down the drunk.

Spur turned to the man beside him. "Morning, John. Thought I'd stop by for a visit."

Captain John Trevarow let out a long held breath, grabbed Spur's hand and shook it, his face breaking into a delighted smile. "McCoy, you have no idea how glad I am to see you."

"I have some idea. Buy you a beer?"

An hour later at the Philadelphia Beer Depot, Spur and Captain Trevarow had corned beef sandwiches and caught up on each other's news.

Spur was surprised how John had aged. He was maybe sixty-two, six-feet tall and now not only thin, but on the gaunt side. His skin color wasn't the best either and Spur watched him carefully as he listened.

"Got into Bridgeport about three years ago when I was moving around. They needed somebody over here who could whip this town into shape. Lord knows I tried. This town has too much money, too many wild women and too much booze. You know there are three breweries in town? *Three of them,* and all turning out more beer than we can drink."

"Place looks prosperous," Spur said.

"Yeah, it is. Looks civilized, too, but it ain't. Some days we average a killing a day. Been a week now without a shooting death. That worries me." Captain Trevarow sipped his beer. "Hell, ten years ago I'd have eaten this town alive. Now, I ain't so fast. I can shoot straight as anybody, but getting the damn thing out of the leather takes me just too damn much time.

"Now, take that slasher drunk up at the cat houses. Probably a right nice gent when he's sober. Trouble is the only time I see these guys is when they're drunk or mad or when they go crazy." Trevarow sighed. "Don't know how much more of it I can take, McCoy. I might be dead right now if you hadn't walked up when you did. It was getting about as nasty as it can before the lead starts to fly."

Spur finished his beer and had another bite of the sandwich. Best corned beef he'd had since he left Chicago.

"John, I understand what you're telling me. If it's any help, you're not the first man to go through this. I've known two of the old gunmen, big names you'd recognize in a second. They both came to a point where they knew if they wanted to go on living much longer, they had to hang up the gun belt.

"One did, he's a popular man now back in Massachusetts. Says he's going to run for the state legislature. The second one couldn't break the chain. He got gunned down in a call out in Virginia City. Some kid who hadn't even started to shave yet beat him and killed him in a half-a-second on one cold winter day."

John Trevarow looked out the window at the dirt

street with piles of horse droppings, each with a thousand flies around it. When his eyes turned back to Spur he seemed to relax a moment. "You're telling me to quit my job, hang up my gun?"

"Not quit your job. This should be a desk job here anyway. Hire whoever you want to for street patrol and door knob checks. Send out three deputies to stop gun fights and to bring in prisoners. That shouldn't be your work. Hell, John, you're a Captain, you're in law management now."

They went on talking and eating their sandwiches. Spur remembered how Trevarow had pulled him out of a tight spot in Kansas six years ago. It had been a small job, pick up a counterfeiter and his plates from the sheriff in a little Kansas town and bring the prisoner and the evidence back to St. Louis.

When Spur went to get the man out of jail, it turned out the gent had six brothers and three brothers-in-law who all owned shotguns and pistols and loved to use them.

For two days they had a standoff with the brothers outside the jail, while Spur, Trevarow and the prisoner remained inside. Nobody could move, nobody would back down. Spur didn't want to get anybody killed over some bad five dollar bills.

At last Spur slipped the gagged prisoner out the back way after midnight and rode half the night to get away from the brothers, while John Trevarow put up a big fuss in the front office of the jail haranguing the men about how they were violating Kansas law and how he'd have them all brought up on charges of obstructing justice and interfering with a peace officer. The charges would get them each five years in the Kansas penitentiary.

By the time John Trevarow had talked himself hoarse, two of the men had slipped around and broke in the back door and found their brother gone. They almost strung up John before he shot one in the shoulder and two more in the legs and backed them down with his own pair of Greeners, one in each hand, with two barrels each and four loads of double ought buck.

As a demonstration he blasted a wooden box in the corner of the jail and shattered it. The in-laws backed down and Spur was well on his way to St. Louis.

Spur finished his sandwich and pushed back from the table as he watched a man come in the front door, look around and go up to the barkeep. His clothes were dusty and there was a line of perspiration on his forehead, as if he'd just come off a long ride.

"Hell, Spur, maybe you're right about hanging up the iron," Trevarow admitted cautiously. "Lord knows I hate to go out where I know I might have to draw fast. But maybe I've done enough law work with a gun. Maybe it's time I concentrate on the other aspects of law and order."

"Then do it. It's what I'd do if I was in the same situation. Damned right I would."

"Captain Trevarow?"

Spur looked up and saw the man he had just watched come in. Spur's hand swung down near his holster automatically.

Trevarow glanced up and nodded. "Yeah, that's me, son. What can I do for you?"

"Deputy at the jail said you was here. My name is Orval Kemp. I'm from Salt Lake City in Utah. I got something to tell you." He looked at Spur.

"It's all right. He can hear whatever it is. Sit down. You had a beer yet since your long ride?"

"No, sir, but I don't drink. I'm sorry to be the

bearer of bad news. I just rode in from Bridgeport along the stage road. Twelve, fifteen miles out on that part where the trail winds up along a gully, my horse acted up. Seemed like he was spooked. I got him calmed down and tied him to a tree and looked around.

"There was stage tracks and all on the road such as it is. Then I saw one set of tracks that cut away from the trail toward the edge of the drop off. Never seen nothing like it before, Sheriff. A stage went over the side!"

"How far down was it?" Spur asked.

"Not more than fifty, sixty feet. That's why I was surprised at first that I didn't see survivors."

"Everyone was killed?" Trevarow asked.

"All shot to death, Sheriff. All men. I counted seven but there might be another one underneath a horse or the coach. All the horses had been shot, too."

Captain Trevarow grabbed his hat and reached for his purse to pay the tab. "Which way was the coach going?"

"Can't be sure, but seemed to be heading for Bridgeport."

"Can you take us back to the spot, Mr. Kemp?"

"Figure I should, Sheriff."

"All men, you say, seven of them, and going toward Bridgeport? Damn! There's only one good explanation and I don't like it." The Captain looked at Spur. "You feel up to a ride in the noonday sun?"

John went to the Wells Fargo office while Spur walked to the Kirkwood Livery Stable to rent a horse and saddle. They all met in front of the U.S. Hotel and John Travarow looked grim. He made the introductions. The new man with him was Ingemar Johnson, manager of the Wells Fargo stage and freight office there in Bodie. His face was set in a deep scowl and he barely acknowledged the introductions.

The four riders turned south on Main and rode out of town up the first slope and along the stage road south and west toward Bridgeport.

Johnson rode ahead with the man who found the wreckage. He asked him a stream of questions, but Kemp knew few of the answers.

Captain Trevarow rode beside Spur. "Johnson is the manager of the Wells Fargo stage. If he's right, those seven men Kemp found could have been Wells Fargo guards."

"Why seven?" Spur stopped. "A gold shipment was on that stage?"

"That's the way we've been sending out gold now for three or four years. Up to a hundred pounds of bullion goes in a strong box, and Wells Fargo guarantees it delivered to the mint in San Francisco in thirty-six hours.

"No passengers are permitted, and they send along seven heavily armed guards and the best driver they have. Never lost a shipment before. But Johnson says it sounds like it could be the stage he sent out last night about four A.M. Nobody ever knows when the gold is being sent, and by midnight hardly anybody is up to see the rig leave from the back of one or another of the mines where it picks up the gold."

"But somebody knew about this one," Spur said. "You figure it's the gold stage?"

"A driver in Bridgeport said the stages going into Bodie are always full these days, almost nobody coming out. Why else would seven men be leaving Bodie except as Wells Fargo guards?"

It took them just over two and a half hours to ride

to the spot on the trail where Kemp stopped. He showed them the drop off and tied up his mount.

Johnson swung off his horse, dropped the reins and slid down the slope to the wreck below.

Almost at once a wail of despair echoed up the canyon.

By the time Spur and Captain Trevarow skidded and slipped down the side of the gully, they found Johnson sitting on a rock with tears streaming down his face.

He nodded when Captain Trevarow asked him if this was the gold shipment stage.

"I knew every one of these men. They were like brothers to me. We'd never lost a guard before on any of our runs out here! Not in six years. Now eight men all at once!"

Spur checked the men he could locate. All had been shot. None of them had weapons. He found the battered strong box and carried it over to Johnson. They could see how the lock had been shot off.

"That's our strong box," Johnson said. "We've got to take the bodies back to Bodie for a Christian burial."

"We can't today, Mr. Johnson," Spur said. "We'll send out a wagon tomorrow to bring them back."

Johnson stared at the face of one of the dead men a dozen feet away. "Eight of them! God, what am I going to tell their wives? What can I tell my superiors? Do I just write them a dispatch saying I lost a $25,000 shipment of gold? My God, that's as much money as I make in fifty years!"

"We better be heading back for Bodie," Captain Trevarow said.

They had to help Johnson climb back up to the horses. All the way on the three hour ride home he kept repeating over and over that all eight of them had been murdered. All eight!

Spur and Captain Trevarow had checked the killing site carefully. There was not a clue as to who had robbed the stage. There were horseshoe tracks, but nothing distinctive. Most had long since been trampled by a stage going each way pulled by four horses and numerous horseback riders. Nothing at the site would help them find the killers.

It was dark by the time the four men rode back into Bodie. Johnson had pulled himself together, and went directly to the Standard Mining Company office to give them the news about their shipment. He never hesitated, it was his job and he would do it without fail.

Spur turned in his mount at the Kirkwood livery and went with Captain Trevarow for a dinner at the U.S. Hotel. Both men were tired. Spur destroyed a one-pound steak with all the side dishes as he listened to John tell him about the town.

"We mushroomed from fifteen-hundred to ten or twelve thousand in about two years. Never seen anything like it. But when you get right down to it, we're only an overgrown gold mining camp. People around here brag that Bodie has absolutely the worst climate in the country. In the summer it's hot and desert dry, and the wind always blows. In the winter it's freezing your balls off cold and usually about six to eight feet of snow. This will never be a resort where city people come to take the mountain air."

"The mines are the only basic industry here then," Spur said. "If the mines all went dry tomorrow, how long would Bodie last?"

Captain Trevarow snorted. "Last? Maybe a year as people used up their savings. Without the mines there's no income. Nothing could survive here. This

31

would be only another mining ghost town.''

They didn't talk long. When the food was gone they went their separate ways. Trevarow had a room at one of the smaller hotels and ate out. He had never married.

Spur said goodnight and walked upstairs to his second floor front room and started to unlock his door. He missed the keyhole with the skeleton key and the door swung inward slowly.

Before the door had opened an inch, Spur had his Colt .45 out of leather and the deadly muzzle led the way as Spur McCoy stepped into his room.

3

Spur pushed the unlocked door to his room inward an inch. At once he saw that a lamp was burning inside. He rammed the door open and stepped to the side of the door jamb where the wall protected him. No shots blasted through the opening. He peered around the door frame and laughed.

"Pretty little Jessica!" Spur drawled as he stepped into his room and closed the door.

A girl sat on the bed reading a magazine. Her shoes were off, her legs crossed and she wore only a thin cotton petticoat. She hugged her knees a minute, big brown eyes staring at him, long blonde hair tousled around her shoulders.

"Hi there, cowboy. It's been a long time." She jumped off the bed and bounced into his arms, her hands tight around his neck. "It's so *good* to see you! It was Salt Lake City, if you've forgotten. I got in a little trouble and you managed to set everything straight and get me a ticket on the stage."

"Three years ago, Jessica."

"I saw your fancy shooting demonstration in Virgin Alley. You always been so good with a six-gun?"

"Helps a guy like me stay alive." He carried her to the bed, kissed her cheek and sat her down. He dropped beside her. "Now, tell me all about what you've been doing, where you've been, and how many marriage proposals you've turned down."

Jessica smiled, then lifted her brows with a little shrug. "Spur McCoy, you know what I've been doing. I've been to Sacramento, San Francisco, Portland and down to San Diego. I love that little town. Now I'm starting to work east again."

"You are a traveling girl. How long have you been in Bodie?"

"Six months. It's a good town to winter over in. They work two or three shifts underground rain, snow, sleet or shine so there's always plenty of money, and customers."

"For as long as the boom lasts. Somebody said there were thirteen-thousand people here now."

"They'll stay as long as the gold holds out," Jessica said. "But not me. Another six months or so and I'll be buying a ticket down to the railroad at Sacramento. I'll hate to leave. I'm working for the best lady I've ever met. Her name is Miss Hetti and she runs the Highgrader House of True Pleasure."

Jessica reached up and kissed his cheek. "Now, you handsome, wonderful man, tell me what you've been doing these past three years."

"You know what I've been doing, working for the government, getting shot at, winning more than losing, not dead yet, and not getting overpaid."

"Short and sweet." Jessica went to her knees on the bed and gracefully lifted the thin petticoat over her head, revealing her sleek figure. She was barely five feet tall, slender, with small hand sized breasts with bright pink areolas and darker nipples that now hardened and rose.

"Business first, Spur McCoy. Remember in Salt Lake I told you I owed you so much I could never repay all of it. Least I can do right now is make you a payment. Then I want to talk, and have a beer, and talk some more."

She pulled his face down to her breasts and maneuvered one to his mouth.

"You have any arguments with that, cowboy?"

Spur bit her nipple gently, felt her respond. "I'm taking you away from your gainful employment."

"Tough titty. I told Miss Hetti about you and she said I had the night off. You've got to meet her, she's a marvel. Almost sixty now and straight and slender and in charge. She won't allow a gun or a knife in the rooms. The gents got to check them in the lobby or they never get upstairs. If I was smart I'd stick with Hetti. She's got six or seven girls who have been with her in two different towns now."

Jessica moved his head to her other breast and sighed. "Hey, I promise not to cry, but you mind me talking a little?"

"Talk away, pretty girl."

"Good. I would have anyway, I always was a big talker. But I've been thinking a lot lately about whoring. As long as I don't get a disease, it ain't hurtin' me none. Oh, I get slapped around sometimes, but Hetti makes whoever does it pay twenty dollars and gives it to the girl.

"Usually it's like I'm just a thing some man uses to get his prick hard so he can pump it off. By that time most of them are snorting and bucking like a range bull anyway and they don't care where they stick it.

"But once in a while a real gent will come in. His
wife is having a baby, or she's gone back east, and
for a half hour I get treated like a lady. Those are the
men who really make love, not just have sex. That's
the way I felt with you in Salt Lake. It was a real
treat. I mean, you even thought about how I was
feeling and what I wanted to do. That . . . that's so
damn unusual."

She pulled his face up to hers. "Nice man, Spur
Charles McCoy." Jessica grinned as he looked up
sharply. "Yep, I know your real given name. Wager
there ain't six people in the whole wild west who
knows your Christian name." Jessica smiled at him
and kissed his cheek.

"Just wondering, nice man, Spur Charles McCoy,
if you'd consider giving a whore like me a real kiss
right on the lips?"

Spur kissed her. He knew more about Jessica than
anyone but her family. She would never be a whore
to him. He kissed her gently, then wet her lips with
his tongue and felt them open. He caught her
shoulders and gently pushed her down on the bed,
suspended himself over her fragile body, and kissed
her again.

She purred softly deep in her throat. When he
eased away from her she opened her eyes, and
blinked away tears. "McCoy, you kiss me about
three more times that way, and I'm going to start
following you around like a puppy dog. I'll hound
you to take me with your wherever you go, and I'll
even learn to shoot a derringer and a little .25 pistol
to help you in your business.

"You just turn me into buttermilk and chocolate
candy and fancy lacework that is so fine!" She
knuckled away moisture from her eyes and traced

the lines of his jaw with one delicate finger. "Damn, McCoy, you turn me into a little girl again. I get to thinking about a cottage of my own with flowers around it and maybe even a white picket fence and a husband and at least two little babies and a buggy out front. Isn't that ridiculous?"

"Not ridiculous at all, Jessica. It's past time you retired and moved to a warm climate and opened a boarding house. San Diego would be a good place. It's growing, and it has a future. You think about it."

She nodded, then pushed Spur away from her, rolled him on his back and sat on the bed as she undressed him. "You remember I liked to peel the clothes off you? I still do.

"You kidding about a boarding house in San Diego? That would take five hundred dollars, maybe even a thousand. I don't have that kind of money. Sure I have some, but not that much."

She stared at him a minute from her deep brown eyes, then she shook her head of blonde hair.

"Now don't try to confuse me when I'm paying off an old debt. I'm going to enjoy making this payment."

When she stripped down his pants and his short underwear, she cooed and bent and kissed his erection.

"Glory! I was afraid maybe you had fucked him down to a nub! Glad to see him so bright and huge!"

Jessica sat on Spur's stomach, straddling him, then bent forward until one breast hung over his mouth. "You see anything you'd like to take a bite of, please go easy. I don't have enough tit to let you chew off much." As she said it she ground her hips against his stiffness and Spur groaned in delight.

She let him chew a moment, then lifted her hips

and moved lower so she could angle his shaft into her.

"As I remember, you like the first one fast and furious," Jessica said.

She settled down on his lance, yelping in satisfaction as it penetrated deeper and deeper inside her. At last she bent and kissed his lips.

"The party is yours, Spur Charles, whenever you want to start."

Spur roared his pleasure and thrust up at her. Then she began bobbing and moving forward as if she were riding a race horse, and at once Spur felt the double action on his shaft.

Jessica supported herself on her knees and elbows as she rode him. Spur felt things moving too quickly. She always had excited him in a few furious moments.

Now he surged upward again and again. Then with one final thrust, he launched his seed into her and again pounded a dozen times before he was empty and panting like one of the steam rigs that lifted the cables that came up from the mile deep gold mines.

Her inner muscles gripped him, massaging the last bits of juice from McCoy. Then she lowered herself to cover him and they both panted and rested.

Five minutes later she lifted off him and sat looking down as his eyes came open.

"You're as fast as a sixteen-year-old boy, you know that?"

"When I grow up I'll do better."

Jessica laughed and it made her eyes light up and one dimple punched in on her cheek. "Spur Charles, you could not possibly get any better. Even if you aren't grown up, I like you this way. Never change."

"Everything changes." He told her about John Trevarow.

"Really? He's got half the men in town still scared of him. They know his reputation. I never even figured that he was slowing down." Jessica frowned. "But his color isn't good. Have you noticed? His skin is kind of pale, unhealthy looking."

"Might be some sickness. Don't let on I talked to you about it. Half this lawman job is having a good reputation with a fast gun. I think he's going to stay in the office most of the time, now."

She jumped off the bed, her breasts bouncing and her bare little bottom jiggling as she hurried to the side of the room and brought out four bottles of beer from a paper bag. They had been cold once from ice from the Bodie ice house. Now they showed sweat stains but were still chilled.

She opened two bottles, gave him one and sat cross legged on the bed beside him tipping the second.

"A boarding house in San Diego? Were you kidding?"

"No. Buy an older house with eight or ten rooms, rent out four or five bedrooms, throw in two meals a day, and you can make a good living. Then if one of your renters takes your fancy, you might even wind up getting married."

"With my luck the second boarder would be an ex-customer from the Highgrader here in Bodie. What would I do then?"

"You'd have a heart to heart talk with the gent, and tell him you'll blow his brains out if his breathes a word of your former life. Most men will be glad to see you making it on the other side."

A far off look came into her brown orbs and she

smiled. "I remember our house back in Cleveland. We had a yard with grass in it and everything. I even had a puppy that grew up into a strange looking mutt that we called Rover. I think he sired about a hundred litters in that neighborhood."

"Think about San Diego."

"A real daydream. Impossible."

"Not really. The stage was robbed of the gold shipment. If you don't know, you would have heard tomorrow. There could be a reward for capturing the robbers. They killed eight men in the process."

"How awful!" She frowned. "A reward?"

"Men who rob and kill often spend lots of money soon afterwards. Watch for anyone in that mood, or talking about lots of money. Sometimes men talk more in a crib than they do in a barroom. Remember, whoever robbed that stage, also killed eight men."

They finished the beers and Spur patted the bed beside him. Jessica curled up beside him.

"Now it's your turn," McCoy said. "Tell me what pleasures you the most, anything you want, any way. It's time for Jessica to have exactly what she wants for a change."

"Glory be, no man ever talked to me that way before."

Spur's hands crept over her body, pausing at the pleasure zones and soon he had her panting.

It was halfway to daylight before they got to sleep that night, and both of them were smiling.

Captain Trevarow had sent a wagon out to the stage robbery site as soon as it was daylight. The wagon rolled into town slightly after noon, and Spur had only just got up and shaved. He let Jessica sleep while he dressed and slipped out the door and arrived at Bodie jail the same time the death wagon did.

"Roll on down to the undertaker," Captain Trevarow said when he looked at the wagon filled with the corpses. "Hooperman will have a field day because most of those men have family in town."

Spur followed the rig to the undertaker and saw the name I.C. Hooperman on the sign outside the door. The place was on an alley down from the jail half a block on Bonanza Street.

Spur watched a short, fat man inspect the cargo.

"Eight!" he said at first, alarmed. Then nodding. "Yes, yes, of course we can take care of them. Have the families been notified? Be sure the Captain tells each family so proper arrangements can be made. They'll want correct clothing and perhaps some extra nice coffins."

He stopped and looked up at Spur. "You must be McCoy. Heard about you costing me gainful employment yesterday. I can't win them all. Name's Hooperman, I. C. Hooperman. Everyone calls me Hoop."

Colt took the surprisingly strong handshake and returned the man's big grin. "Deadly business you're in, Hoop."

"Not as deadly as yours. You drop them, I pick them up and plant them. But you know, none of them have grown yet!" Hooperman slapped his thigh and roared with laughter at his own small joke.

"Let's hope they don't sprout all over the cemetery. That would be a mess."

Hooperman laughed again, this time until tears came to his eyes. "By damn! Glad we got somebody in town with a sense of humor. I get tired of trying

to make jokes to folks who don't appreciate them.
Fact is, I always wanted to be an entertainer. Get up
and tell jokes and funny stories and regale the
crowd. Fancied myself with some show troop going
from town to town.

"Then I had to help in the family business." He
pointed around him at the undertaking parlor's back
room. "My dad died two years later and I had a
ready made business. I've been laying out folks and
getting them dressed in their Sunday best ever
since."

He helped the men carry in one of the dead guards
and came back panting.

"Hey, McCoy, did I tell you the one about Doc
Rogers? He told his patient, Herman, that he had
only six months to live and then gave him a bill for
ten dollars. Herman was shocked by the news but
told Doc Rogers he could only pay him a dollar a
month. 'In that case, you have ten months to live,'
Doc Rogers said."

Hooperman doubled over howling with laughter.
Spur joined in and when they both recovered, Spur
motioned to the bodies.

"I'm working with Captain Trevarow. If you see
anything unusual with the bodies, or find any
papers on them we should know about, be sure to
send us a message."

"Deed I will, McCoy. Good to know there's a man
in town who can still laugh."

Spur went back to the jail and talked with John
Trevarow.

"Not much farther along then we were last night,
'cept for one thing." He pointed to his gunbelt and
the well worn .44 that now hung on a coat hook on
the wall. "Decided to leave the blamed thing over

there as long as I can. Maybe forever," Trevarow said.

"Good, we're making real progress in keeping you alive. Also, I met the local humorist, Hocp. He's going to be busy today."

"He'll have to use blocks of ice from the ice house. That'll be four funerals today and three tomorrow. Right, he's gonna be damn busy."

"Talked to the Wells Fargo people this morning, yet?"

"Nope. Hoped you'd want to go along. I got this government agent in town, I might as well make good use of him."

"Fact is, this is close enough to government business that I can be official, since the gold was heading for the United States mint in San Francisco. Let's go."

Ingemar Johnson was in no better a frame of mind that morning than he had been when they rode back from the death scene the evening before. He had shadows under his eyes, and jumped at every little noise. His hands wrapped around a large coffee cup and he sipped at the brew frequently.

"I sent a long letter to the company on the morning stage. As soon as the stage hits Sacramento, they'll send a wire to San Francisco. Then we wait for word. I'm not sure what else I have to do—besides find the murdering bastards, get the gold back, and then hang all of them!"

"Wondering if there was anything you know that we could start working with, Mr. Johnson," Spur said. "I know your security is tight. But you've been shipping gold out of Bodie now for two or three years at least. A lot of people must know how you do it. Have you had any unhappy employees lately who

have been discharged, caught stealing, got mad at
the company and quit? Anything like that?''

''No!''

''Take your time, Mr. Johnson, and think it
through. Every company I've ever seen has had a
few unhappy workers. It's normal. A driver, a
freight man, maybe a guard who would know the set
up.''

Johnson sipped the coffee. Spur saw a half empty
pint whiskey bottle in a partly opened desk drawer.
No wonder Johnson loved his coffee this morning.

''All right, I'll think about it. Go back over the
records. I'm . . . I'm still so damn angry . . . .''

He walked to the window taking the coffee cup
with him. After two sips he came back.

''You're right. Somebody knew the gold was going
out. They had to. Here at our firm the people who
knew were me and one clerk. We have to give the
guards four hours notice of a run, so that means
seven more knew about it, and the driver. But it
seems highly unlikely that one of them would tip off
a robber who would then kill the inside man.''

''Means the share of gold is that much bigger for
the survivors,'' Captain Trevarow said.

''My God! I'm not used to dealing with that kind
of humanity. I just can't imagine it. Whoever it was
knew exactly where to stop the stage. The climb up
that hill means the rig has to come almost to a dead
stop to make the corner and then head up the slope.''

''Who at the mine knew about the shipment?''
Spur asked.

''Oh, the superintendent, of course. The head
bookkeeper, a trusted man, and I'd say at least one
man in the bullion storage area. At least three of
them.''

''So ten of your people, and three at the mine,''

Spur said. "I'd tend to go along with you on the guards and the driver. Any holdup means a risk for those on board. That leaves your clerk and the three at the mine."

"Could we talk with your clerk, please," Trevarow asked.

"Of course. He's been with us since the start. Six years we've been struggling here. I'd trust him with my virgin daughters and my wife's jewelry. I'll have him come in."

Ten minutes later they finished talking to the clerk. He had the imagination and ambition of a dried prune. Spur saw no way possible that the man could have planned the robbery or been any part of it. He was about fifty years old, a bookkeeper and clerk, and that was his whole life. Matching sets of figures in books were the most exciting elements in the universe to him.

"Where do your guards assemble?" Spur asked.

"They don't. We pick them up one at a time along the route. By the time we get to the mine we have our six men inside."

"That's smart. Do you always leave at four A.M.?"

"No, we go as early as first darkness, and as late as five A.M. It's different each run."

"How many trips a month with gold?"

"Depends on production. Last month we made four trips. This month it will probably be six."

"Is it always $25,000 in gold?"

"No, but never less than that. Never more than $50,000 which is about 150 pounds of bullion. More than that won't fit into our standard strong box."

Captain Trevarow stood. "Ingemar, is there anything else you need to tell us?"

Johnson shook his head, drained the coffee and

sighed. "Wish to hell I could point a finger at the traitor, but I can't."

Outside the stage office, Spur looked up the slope. "Is it about time for us to go talk to the men at the Standard Mining Company?"

"I'd say so. Right now the head man we should see is one of the Cook brothers, Dan by first name. He handles most of the above ground end of the Standard. I'm sure he'll want to meet with us."

As they walked up the hill toward the Standard stamp mill, the clang, clang, clang of the metal rods pounding down on the gold and silver ore to crush it became louder and louder. Spur realized he had heard the sound before and quickly that morning had relegated it to a normal background sound and dismissed it.

It was what every resident of Bodie had done. It was only when the stamping mills stopped pounding, that the Bodie people looked around and asked each other what had happened.

The Standard Mining Company's office was situated east of the stamp mill and slightly up hill. Inside, the sound of the mill was muffled, and when they walked into Dan Cook's office, heavy draperies on the windows reduced the sound even more.

Dan Cook smiled at them and held out his hand for the introduction. When he heard the name he nodded.

"Yes, Mr. McCoy. I've been reading about you in some of my reports. You work with the government in some sort of law agency, and you are greatly active in the West. I assure you what I have heard is all good.

"I'd assume you gentlemen are here about the robbery. Tragic, just tragic. Eight souls blasted into oblivion that way. Do you have any leads about who did it?"

"We were hoping you could help us there, Mr. Cook," Spur said. "Who here at the Standard knew the shipment was going out, and who loaded the gold?"

"Surely, you don't think . . ." Cook stopped. "Yes, of course, if we don't know who was involved, then everyone must be suspect. I understand. I ordered the shipment. My head clerk, Mr. Vance, did the paperwork, and a trusted employee in the retort room and vault, Niles Ogden, removed the actual bullion from the vault and put it in the strongbox and signed it on the stage. The driver signed a receipt, which I have here for the seventy-five pounds of gold bullion."

"Just you three?" Captain Trevarow asked.

"Yes. Never more. If the hour is too late, I usually load the gold myself. I try never to ask an employee to do something I won't do myself."

"Did anyone outside see the gold being loaded?" Trevarow asked.

"Wouldn't be normal that they would, that time of night. It isn't a shift change. Doubt if anyone noticed. Rigs go charging around here all the time with goods, and wood."

"Seems reasonable," Spur said. "It looks like the way the robbery was planned, the men must have known in advance when the gold would go out, rode into position, and waited for the rig. Just witnessing the gold being loaded wouldn't allow the robbers time to beat the stage to the robbery site."

"Is there anything else you can tell us, Mr. Cook?" Trevarow asked.

"Not that I can think of. The gold was insured,

guaranteed delivery by Wells Fargo, so it isn't a loss. But we're shocked by the deaths of the eight men on the stage. We'll do everything we can to bring the murderers to justice."

"Mr. Cook, could we look at your retort room and the vault, and would you show us, physically, how the gold is moved from there to where the stage sat that night?"

Cook did. It proved nothing for Spur, and gave him no new ideas as to how the information could have come into the wrong hands. The more he thought of it, the more he realized that there had to be a traitor here, a betrayer of the confidentiality of the shipment of gold. But who?

The two law men walked back toward town, moving to the side of the street to avoid a convoy of huge freight wagons loaded down with firewood.

"That's the lifeblood of our town," Captain Trevarow said. "As you can see, we grow no firewood anywhere around here. It all must be freighted in from the Bridgeport area and north of there. The more people who move here, the richer the wood haulers get. If this keeps up much longer, wood will be worth more per pound than silver or gold!"

"They use it to produce the steam for the mills and lift works on the mines, and to heat the houses in winter?" Spur asked.

"We don't have any coal here, so we use wood. Last winter one of my neighbors kept telling me that the man next door to him kept stealing wood off his wood pile. Hard to prove something like that. The man said just wait, he'd get proof.

"That night my neighbor split up a new pile of wood and hollowed out one piece, filled it with black powder, then glued it together. Along about midnight the house next door blew up when the stolen wood in the heating stove burned down to the black powder. That was the last time that gent ever stole a stick of wood.''

They passed more wood rigs heading for the stamping mill, got back to Wood Street and headed for Main. Just after they turned past the U. S. Hotel a young man ran into the street and waved at Spur.

"Hey there, fast gun. Hear you think you're pretty good with that tied down iron.''

The speaker was not much over twenty, wore a fancy shirt with button down pockets and a big silver belt buckle, jeans and cowboy boots. A black, flat topped hat perched on his head.

Spur and Captain Trevarow angled away from the man but he ran in front of them and fired a shot in the air.

"Hey you, the tall, ugly one with the mutton chop sideburns and moustache. The one who says his name's McCoy. Can you talk, or are you too much of a coward to look a real man in the eye?''

Spur turned and eyed the young man. He was thirty feet away.

"I'm McCoy, and I'm not half as drunk as you are, little boy. Why don't you go home and tell your mama to wash out your mouth with soap.''

The young man colored, saw some people watching, and let his right hand hover over his tied down six-gun.

"You just bought yourself a gunfight, McCoy. I can take you, I'm twice as fast as you are. Only one way to prove it.''

Spur laughed. "Boy, you been reading too many of them dime novels about the West? You really think you're good with that iron?''

"Better'n you, old man.''

"You got twenty dollars in your pocket?'' Spur

asked.

"You damn well know it."

"Good. I've got no reason to kill you. So we'll set up a little contest." Spur flipped a double gold eagle in the air and caught it. "Here's my twenty, where's yours? We'll let Sheriff Trevarow here hold the money."

"What the hell you talking about?"

"What's your name, son?"

"Quade, Gerry Quade. A name everybody's gonna know cause I gunned down fast gun Spur McCoy."

"Not quite. We do it this way. We set up two bottles on a fence, pace off thirty feet, and on a signal we both draw and shoot at our bottles. The one who breaks his bottle first, wins the twenty dollars. The best thing about this is you'll still be alive."

"You don't have a chance of beating me, McCoy."

Spur snorted. "Kid, I've seen twenty just like you. Half of them are dead by my gun or somebody else's they challenged. Why don't you want to live long enough to grow up? Make you a deal. You break your bottle first, and I'll let you have a go at me, no rules, a call out shoot down. Agreed?"

"Damn right!"

Captain Trevarow took the young man's twenty dollars, then found two quart sized whiskey bottles and sat them on a fence in back of the U.S. Hotel down by Bodie Creek. Then he paced off thirty feet from the bottles and drew a scar on the ground with his boot.

Quade snorted as he looked at the distance.

"Thirty feet," Spur said. "If that's too far we can move closer."

"Shoot, old man, don't talk."

Spur nodded at Trevarow.

"All right, both of you take your places and get your stance. Don't touch your gun butt. When I call out FIRE, both of you draw and fire. The one who breaks his bottle first, wins."

He let the men settle down on their marks.

"Ready. Both ready? Set. Both set? FIRE!"

Spur's draw was clean, smooth, a blur as his .45 fired, blasting his bottle into a hundred pieces before the other man's weapon cleared leather. Spur fired again shattering the second bottle. He holstered his weapon and turned toward the young man.

"Welcome to the land of the living, Gerry Quade. Next time you challenge a man, make sure you're not half drunk, and make sure you see him shoot before you bet your life. Today you would have lost."

Spur and Captain Trevarow walked away watching the young man as he slowly pushed his unfired .44 into leather. Trevarow handed Spur the two twenty dollar gold pieces.

Two men hurried up, grabbed Quade by the arm and walked him away down the street in the other direction.

"Damn, Quade, you idiot, you almost got yourself killed right there," one of the young men said to his friend.

That was when Spur noticed that Captain Trevarow was not wearing his six-gun. Good, Spur thought, then returned to the problem at hand. Who knew about the gold shipment, and where were the killers right now?

4

Spur walked the streets of Bodie that afternoon trying to figure out who set up the robbery. The best suspects were the two bookkeepers and the bullion man at the Standard. But he'd met all three and not one seemed like the type.

Of course, when fifty years of wages are involved, a lot of normal men can go off the deep end.

Bodie was turning into a real little frontier town. The more people who crowded into a place, the more people it took to handle the needs of all those bodies. They needed wood, they had to have food from the outside, thousands of horses and mules were involved to haul in the goods and provide all those necessary services.

There were freight wagons by the hundreds to haul supplies and gold ore to the stamping mills. Three blacksmiths in town did little except make horseshoes and nail them onto unshod hooves. Bodie had a little of everything now, even jewelry stores, fancy ladies' wear shops and one hat store.

The whole town was built of Jeffrey pine, which was loaded with pitch. Much of the lumber that built Bodie came from the Mono Lake mills to the south. The stores were shoulder to shoulder down Main Street and close together over most of the rest of the town. Spur shuddered at what would happen if one of them caught fire.

The residents had thought the same thing and had erected a fire house just down from the Occidental Hotel on Main. Bodie had plenty of water in case of a bad fire.

Spur leaned against a building on Main and let the warm August sun soak into his bones. Before long the snow would be flying in Bodie, there would be ten or twelve feet of snow and the temperature could drop to 30 even 40 degrees below zero. To add further injury, the wind gusts in a storm could whip up to a hundred miles an hour. In spite of the warm sun, McCoy shivered. He had no intentions of staying in Bodie for the winter snow sliding sports.

The idea that had sparked in his mind an hour ago grew and blossomed and Spur kicked away from the wall and walked down to the Wells Fargo office. Ingemar Johnson, the depot manager, ushered him into his private office and closed the door.

"Any ideas who could have let out the information about the shipment?" Spur asked.

Johnson shook his head.

"Then I have an idea. I want to sign on as a guard on the next gold shipment. When is another one scheduled?"

Johnson scowled. "Is this a good idea?"

"Best way to find out who hit the stage is to stop the next attack, beat them back with firepower and follow the attackers back to their lair. If we capture them, one of them eventually will talk, even if it's to save his own neck from stretching a half-inch of hemp.''

Johnson stared at the letter he was writing to one of the dead men's widows. He took a deep breath, scrubbed a hand over his face and nodded.

"I guess we have to try it. You'll be notified four hours ahead like the other guards. Fact is, I'm having trouble hiring guards now. I've jumped the pay to five dollars a day, but still there are few takers.''

Johnson dropped the pen on his desk and drank from his coffee cup. "Damn! but I hate writing letters to these new widows. It's almost like I was in the war again.''

Spur said he understood the feeling, bowed out of the office and remembered that he hadn't had any food since he got up about noon. He picked one of the smaller restaurants and ordered the special of the day, beef stew, Bodie style. It was the best stew he'd ever eaten with whole potatoes, long carrots, lots of parsnips and tomatoes, chunks of cabbage and half a dozen other vegetables.

At four-thirty that afternoon a messenger found Spur and gave him a sealed envelop. Inside he found this message:

"Meet the Wells Fargo stage tonight at Wood and Union Streets near the Standard at 8 P.M. You'll be paid $5 a day as a guard. Yes, a shipment goes out just after darkness tonight.''

Spur rode shotgun on the gold stage since nobody else would. Johnson had met them at the Bodie mine and explained that they would be taking the regular route for the gold stage: out the road northwest to

Aurora, Nevada, then to Wellington, Gardnerville and on to Carson City. From there it went across to San Francisco's U.S. Mint.

Johnson told Spur that he varied the route from time to time hoping to change the pattern enough to keep the shipments safe.

When they picked up the gold at the Bodie mine, Spur and the other six guards watched the surrounding area, but nothing moved, and no mine employees were near. They hoisted the strong box into the front boot, the men climbed inside and Spur went on the high front seat beside the driver. Then they charged quietly into the night.

The first hour went by swiftly. Inside the coach it was quiet, but the men had been instructed not to sleep, and to watch out the windows at all times.

Spur soon caught the trick of staying on the swaying, jolting high seat by bracing his feet and knees as he kept looking around on the moonless night. He could see less than fifty feet in any direction.

Canute Edwards handled the reins for the team of six like the veteran he was. There were hills steep enough on this run for six horses. Canute had been driving stages for nearly twenty years, he proudly told Spur.

"Started out back in fifty-nine in Missouri. Not much to worry about back there, mostly getting talked to death by some up top passenger. Carried sixteen on one trip. One gent kept getting drunker and drunker until he finally fell off the top. He rolled down a hill, but he was so drunk, he never even knew he fell."

The stage didn't go through the middle of Aurora, didn't stop at the Wells Fargo depot there. It would be a tipoff to any robber to see seven armed men on a stage and moving at night. They skirted the little Nevada town and rushed back on the road north to Wellington.

Spur cradled the Remington double barreled shotgun in his arms as he scanned the way ahead.

Canute kept up a steady stream of chatter. "Not much chance of anybody jumping us along here. We got fifteen miles of open country. Then we could have a spot or two where some ratfaces could make a try at us. My guess is we go through without even a mean look from anybody tonight. Hear you're some special government man out here to hang these killers?"

Spur put the Remington in a bracket inside the seat and picked up the Spencer seven shot rifle the company provided. He felt more at home with the Spencer. He'd save the scattergun for close range work.

If he lived that long. Spur knew the shotgun guard on a stage was the first target of holdup killers. The second victim was the driver or the lead horse, depending on the angle and the situation. But the shotgun guard went first. He lifted his brows as he listened to Canute explain how the stage coach driver used to be the toast of the town.

"Hell, when I was younger I could have me any of the pretty women in town when I'd whip in on a stage and end my run. They just seemed to think it was glamorous and dangerous and somehow very thrilling. For ten years I thought they were thrilling too, then I got married for a spell and she stopped all the catting around. Mostly."

When they came to the first heavily wooded section, Spur tensed, but there was no attack. They wound up the steepest grade on the run and again came through without any trouble.

Three days later Spur rode back to Bodie with the other guards in a regular Wells Fargo stage free of charge. There had been no trouble; the new driver and guards took over in Carson City for the run to San Francisco.

Spur slumped in Captain Trevarow's office.

"Everything quiet here?"

"About as usual. Two knifings, twenty-two drunks slept overnight, six shootings but they were such bad shots that only one man was wounded." Trevarow shifted uneasily in his chair, toyed with a five dollar gold piece and shrugged.

"Hell, you'll find out soon enough. Logan Wilde is in town."

"Wilde, *the* Logan Wilde? The same man you had a small situation with in Cheyenne about ten years ago?"

"Same backshooting bastard. He must have got out of prison. I'm surprised some jealous husband or some honest gambler hasn't pumped six slugs into his worthless carcass by now."

"He's in Bodie. Does he know you're here?"

"Yes. He came here to find me."

"Wilde must be in his fifties now."

"He's fifty-one and bragging about it. Claims he's as fast now as he ever was. He's been throwing up a pint whiskey bottle with his right hand, drawing with his right and shooting the bottle before it hits the ground."

"That's not much."

"We know that, but it's showy, and he's got damned near the whole town in his pocket. When he thinks he's scared me enough, he'll come around. I still haven't put on my gunbelt. Just what the hell am I supposed to do, McCoy?"

"The first thing is to keep your six-gun on the shelf. Don't wear it and don't let him goad you into a fight. Any way you can have your deputies arrest him?"

"He's carefully staying clean. Not even cheating at cards, just brags a lot, tells great stories about his exploits. No way we can touch him."

"Maybe I could rile him a little, get him . . ."

Trevarow held up his hand. "No sir! Not a chance. I don't want you anywhere near this man. I know how fast he was. No telling how fast he still is. I've seen you shoot, but I'm no judge of a thousandth of a second anymore. That could be the difference between living and dying. I'll figure out something."

"He won't wait around long."

"I know that, damnit!" John Trevarow shook his head. "Sorry, Spur . . . sorry."

"You have time to go over for a beer?"

"No. I've been staying out of the saloons last couple of days."

"John, there's sixty-five drinking spots in town. What's the chances of you and Wilde being in the same one at the same time?"

"Depends how hard Wilde looks for me, and how many men he hired to tip him off when I walk in."

"Yeah. Guess you figured out the ride to Carson City was a complete bust. We didn't even see a jackrabbit, let alone get held up."

"Way it goes in law work. You been at it long enough to know you got to be patient."

"True. I'm gonna go have a couple of beers, get the stage dust out of my throat."

John Trevarow didn't look up as Spur left. It took McCoy twelve stops before he found Logan Wilde. He was shorter than Spur had remembered. He'd seen the lawman/outlaw/showman twice before, once when he was town marshal of a small place in Kansas, and again with a small wild west show out of Cheyenne.

Wilde was not more than five-feet seven. He looked his fifty years, with a pot belly and a sag to his features, especially around his eyes. He wore his hat in the saloon, cowboy style, as contrasted to most of the miners who watched him. When he came out of his chair there was a momentary hitch as he favored one leg, then he shifted his weight and grinned at the crowd.

Now he had fifteen drinkers around him lapping up his tall tales of being a fast gun desperado. He even told them about the one bank robbery he and two other guys pulled back in Nebraska ten years ago and nobody ever figured out who did it.

Spur bought a beer and drank it from the bottle, watching the show from a distance. Then Wilde had the apron bring out an empty beer keg and set it on a chair next to the alley wall.

"Now, gents, my bet is that I can hear a call to fire, draw and shoot and hit the keg before you can count off three seconds. Any takers."

Wilde looked around the saloon in astonishment. "You mean there's isn't a single man here who'll risk a thin one dollar gold piece to see me shoot the cork out of that empty beer keg?"

At last one man held up his hand waving a dollar bill.

"Well, now, that's a start. Who wants to be the counter? You have to say: One thousand and one,

one thousand and two, one thousand and three. Say it out loud at just about that pace.''

The barkeep walked over and said he would give the word to fire, if somebody would count. He took the better's dollar bill and one from Wilde and belched.

"Hell, I'll do the counting," a man at the end of the bar said. "I can still get to three."

"I'll tell you when to fire," the barkeep said, evidently bored, maybe because he did this same routine a dozen times a day. "You ready, Wilde?"

Wilde stretched his right arm, took an eighteen inch stance facing the keg from twenty feet and nodded.

"Fire!"

The counter started: "One thousand and one . . ."

Wilde's hand darted to his holster, his finger lanced into the trigger housing, he pivoted the weapon up still in the holster and fired before the man could say one thousand and three. He used a trick swivel holster with a hole in the end to fire through. Spur had seen them before, but never used quite so efficiently.

Wilde took the dollar and grinned. "Now, gents, just to make it more interesting, I'll give you five to one odds that I can't hit the barrel before our counter gets to one thousand and two! Do I have a few takers? I can't try this without considerable money being on the table."

This time a dozen men crowded up to the poker table and began putting down money. One man bet twenty dollars. Each man talked with the barkeep and when the amount was settled, the apron put the money on the table and covered each stack with poker chips from his pocket.

"Any more sports want to see me go home without my shooting irons as I try to pay off these ridiculously high odds?"

One more man came down and bet five dollars.

The barkeep checked his pad of paper. "That's eighty seven dollars bet, Mr. Wilde. If you lose, you'll owe me four hundred and thirty-five dollars."

Wilde pretended to sweat. He wiped his brow, looked at the men.

"Can we cut those odds to three to one?" he asked.

They shouted him down.

"Come on, shoot!" somebody said.

"Yeah, I'm buying a new rifle with my winnings!" another called.

Wilde looked at them. "Damn you! You didn't have to bet so much. Hell, I'll remember Bodie as the town where I lost my shirt, my purse, and my favorite gun. Where can I get four hundred and thirty-five dollars?"

"Shut up and shoot!" A heavy voice called from the crowd.

Wilde shrugged, wiped sweat off his brow again, then settled his Stetson in place and flexed his hand.

"Come on, fast draw, don't let us down now!" Wilde shouted.

The barkeep seemed bored, not caught up in the drama of the moment.

"You ready, Mr. Wilde?" the apron asked.

"Yeah, in a minute. Let me concentrate. I'll nod when I'm set, then you call out, and the counter starts counting." He took a deep breath, shook both hands, then flexed his right over his gun butt. Now Spur saw that the holster was cut a little lower than most to allow his finger to slide into the trigger housing as his thumb cocked the hammer.

Wilde nodded.

"Fire!"

"One thousand and one, one thousan . . ."

The six-gun fired, the bullet thunked into the beer keg and the audience applauded, then booed.

Wilde turned, concern on his face. "Mr. Counter, how did you count me?"

"Count? I got to a thousand on the two but never said two. I'm afraid that you've won."

The men jeered the decision. Wilde picked up the eighty seven dollars, gave the chips back to the barkeep and ordered a beer for every bettor. As the barkeep passed the man who counted, Spur saw him slip the man a five dollar bill. There was no way that Wilde could have lost the contest with the fix in for the counter.

Spur finished his beer and drifted outside. It was mid afternoon. The town bustled with heavy hauling rigs, bringing in supplies for the winter. It was an eighteen mile haul to Aurora, and about the same to Bridgeport. Teamsters shouted and swore at their mules and horses.

One rig with sixteen mules hauling it rolled down Main Street heading for the Boone General Store and warehouse at Green and Main. The teamster yelling at the mules said he had 40,000 pounds of goods in his two wagons and hadn't even made a dent in the boxes waiting to come in.

People expected a long, hard winter. One old timer said he got his signals from the jackrabbits. He hadn't seen one now for two months. He claimed they all had headed for the Owens Valley fifty miles to the south.

Spur stepped off the boardwalk and out from

under the overhanging second story porches that covered the boardwalk in front of most stores the length of Main Street. He saw Captain John Trevarow heading across the street a half block down. Almost at the same time he heard a man laugh and looked to the boardwalk on the other side.

Logan Wilde stepped into the dust of the street and pushed his black coat back so it exposed his .45 in the trick holster.

"Damn my hide if it ain't that low down skunk I've been looking for, John Trevarow. You wouldn't be hiding behind a badge, would you, yellow John?"

The two men stopped twenty feet apart.

"I'm gonna kill you, Trevarow, in a clean, honest draw and shootout."

"I'm not armed," Trevarow said. "I don't intend to be armed. You shoot me now and my friends here will see you hang for murder."

"Get a gun, you asshole!" Wilde snapped. He walked closer. "You want everyone to know what a coward you are?" He shouted the words so all could hear.

"I'll get a gun for you, you son of a whore!" He looked behind him. "Bring me a six-gun somebody," he bellowed.

Nobody moved.

"Bring me a gun, now, dammit!" Wilde screamed. At last a man came forward and handed a weapon to Wilde. The gunman walked up to Trevarow and pushed the barrel inside the lawman's belt on his right side.

Wilde turned his back to Trevarow and walked away twenty feet and spun around.

"Now, you gut shooting bastard, you have no excuse. You can draw or not, up to you. I'm calling you out for killing my brother by shooting him in the back in Kansas. I'm counting to three, then I'm going to kill you. Draw if you want to, or don't draw. No jury would convict me long as you have a weapon in your belt."

Wilde turned to the crowd that had assembled as if by magic. More than a hundred people watched in silence from a safe distance to each side of the gunmen.

"You all see that he has a weapon. If he doesn't want to defend himself, that's his funeral, right?"

A few in the crowd shouted agreement. Most stood, wondering what would happen. Spur began to move toward the pair.

"Wait a minute," Spur called.

Wilde ignored him. "One!" Wilde shouted. He adjusted his rig, moved his feet a little farther apart.

"Two," the gunman called.

Spur started to run but he knew he'd be too late. Then as he watched in astonishment, a woman surged from the boardwalk less than two feet behind Wilde and charged at him from the side. At the last moment she brought out a six-inch hunting knife and swiped it at Wilde's throat.

As if the whole thing had happened in frozen bits of time, Spur saw the blade slash across Wilde's throat. Immediately a spurt of red blood shot ten feet into the air and fell to the dusty street.

The woman raised the knife to cut him again, but Wilde turned and looked at her in shock and surprise. He tried to bring his gun hand up to his pistol, but spurt after spurt of rich red blood gushed from his right carotid artery. Four seconds after the slashing, Wilde dropped to his knees. His right hand came up to try to stop the flow of blood which now sprayed out in a steady stream.

Spur ran forward but it felt as if he were struggling through waist deep water.

Wilde looked up at the woman once more, then his eyes rolled back in their sockets and he fell face down into the pulverized dust of Main Street.

Spur charged up to the spot, took one look at Wilde and knew he had bled to death. He held out his hand and the woman gave him the knife, then she collapsed in Spur's arms.

John Trevarow hurried up, touched the man's throat on the uncut side and shook his head. He looked at Spur's unconscious burden.

"Take her over to the jail. We'll have to find out why she did that." Spur looked down at one of the old time fast guns and headed for the jail. Sometimes the Bad Men of Bodie turned out to be human after all.

It was two long blocks up to the jail and before they reached there, the woman he carried revived.

"I can walk," she said, surprising Spur. "We going to jail?"

"Yes, ma'am."

"I figured we would. Been planning to kill Logan ever since I seen him in town. He's so careful. Knew once he started counting he would be concentrating on his draw, that's when I could get close enough to him. He's dead, isn't he?"

"Yes, but you better not say anything else until Captain Trevarow talks to you."

The sheriff borrowed a horse and rode beside them the last block to the jail.

They gave the woman a wet cloth for her forehead, and sat her in the best chair in Trevarow's office. Then the Captain decided it was time to begin. "Your name?"

"Captain, you know me. I'm Sweetheart."

"I mean your real name, the one your mother gave you."

"Oh. Glynnis Funkhouser."

"How old are you?"

"Twenty-eight."

"You work in Virgin Alley?"

"Yeah, I'm a whore. That's why I killed Logan. We was married once. I still got the certificate in my gear. Still married, far as I could tell. The bastard sold me into a whore house in New Orleans. They needed northern girls down there. Locked us up every night. We was all prisoners. He got a thousand dollars for me but he promised that he'd be back in a month and pay off the thousand and we could move on. Fucker never came back. Never had no idea of coming back."

"He was a white slaver?"

"Don't know, but he sold me to a whore house. I finally got away . . . had to stab a man to get out and then I run and run, but the only thing I could do to make a living by then was to lay on my back. That was six years ago. So here I am. I swore that if I ever saw Logan Wilde again, I'd kill the bastard. So I saw him and I waited, and I killed him!"

Spur looked at Captain Trevarow.

"Let's go find that marriage license, Mrs. Wilde. That will help us believe the rest of your story."

They found it in her current house of employment on Maiden Lane. Spur checked the date. It had been issued in the state of Mississippi on November 9, 1873. It was signed and witnessed and looked as legal as possible.

John thought on the matter for a few seconds, then waved Sweetheart away. "The whole story will be in the next issue of the Bodie Standard newspaper. As far as I'm concerned, it's a matter of self defense . . . with some time between the death dealing deed by the deceased before the attacker had a chance to return in kind."

Spur grinned. Western mining camp justice might be a bit strange at times but it was wonderful.

"If the general population does not complain about my decision, we'll consider the matter closed. But, if enough of the folks in town put up a protest, we'll have to have the judge go over the matter next time he's in town."

Sweetheart kissed Captain Trevarow tenderly on this cheek and smiled.

"I guess I'm sad I killed him, but what he done to me is a bit worse than what he got. I'd say he's the one who come out ahead. Leastwise nobody is gonna shoot him down as he gets older and slower on the draw."

Captain Trevarow stared at Sweetheart a minute.

"First thing you know we'll be giving you a medal for saving the poor slob a fate worse than death." He turned and walked out of the sporting house without another word.

Sweetheart shrugged, Spur waved at her not to worry about it and caught up with the local law.

"Don't say a word!" Trevarow snapped when Spur fell in stride beside him. "On this one I'm damned either way. I let her off scot free, and the blabbermouths will say I did it cause she just saved my life. I bring her up on charges, and the other side will say she rid Bodie of a card cheat and cad and ne'er-do-well and our fair city is much better off without the likes of him smelling up the place."

"Yeah, you got the tough part, John. All I have to do is solve eight murders and try to find out who stole cash money that is equal to fifty years of my pay."

Captain John Trevarow of the Sheriff's office snorted and turned in at his office as Spur McCoy continued toward his hotel and what he hoped would be a nice bath in a real bathtub with soap and big fluffy white towels.

5

Colt had his bath. Two men brought a large copper tub to his room and four buckets of hot water and three of cold. When the water cooled off he got out.

That evening he had a lonesome dinner at the U.S. Hotel dining room and then walked the town, investigating some of the 65 saloons he hadn't been in. Half of them had dance hall girls and rooms upstairs.

From all the wild stories he'd heard the last couple of years, Spur figured there'd be a gunfight in every saloon every night. Wasn't true. Most of the patrons were worried only about having a drink or two, or winning at faro or poker or one of the other games of chance.

It was nearing midnight when Spur tried one more saloon, the Gymnasium, ordered a beer and stood at the bar to watch the rituals. Spur was about to leave when he saw a man walk in the door and look around. His six gun was tied low on his left hip and his left hand never strayed far from the polished butt.

Spur knew the signs, a gunman pure and deadly. The man looked around and walked past the game tables until he grunted with satisfaction and stopped in front of one. He reached down, caught the poker table by one hand and tipped it over through a vacant chair. The two men at the table came to their feet sputtering and screaming.

One of the players looked at the gunman and then slowly backed away. The second poker player quieted and watched the small drama.

"Been looking for you now for two years, Yates," the gunman said in a quiet voice. "Usually back-shooters like you don't live this long."

"I don't know who you are, Mister," the player said. He still backed up, his glance darting toward the door, but he must have decided it was too far away to try for. He came against the bar and could move no farther.

"Never seen you before, Mister, now back off," the card player yelled in protest.

"Not a chance, Yates. Vern Yates is the name you used to use over at Denver. You figured you was a big man back there, remember?"

The gunman stood lean and ready, nearly six feet tall with a slender frame, a thin face and deep set, sharp black eyes. He wore a fancy gambler's shirt and vest under a black jacket, dressed up for Bodie.

"Never been to Denver," Yates said, his voice unsteady.

"Your wife Belle remembered me. I just stopped by at your house. That woman of yours is good fucking, better than most of the whores I've used."

Yates growled, his hand moved toward the gun on

his belt, but he didn't draw, never even touched the weapon.

"I got no fight with you, Deadman. Sure, I was in the posse, but I never fired a shot at you."

"Two other gents I conferred with say you lie. They say all three of you fired up a storm, but you was the only one to hit me. Know they didn't lie. Men on their deathbeds always tell the truth.

"Right now, Yates, we settle accounts. All you have to do to clear your name is go for your gun, draw and shoot me dead. That is, if you can."

Yates began edging for the door.

"One more step and I gun you down right here whether you draw or not, asshole Yates! You want a chance to live, you do it like a man and draw!"

By that time the men in the saloon had all moved to each side of the pair who stood about fifteen feet apart. Wild shots killed more innocent bystanders than participants in these affairs and the onlookers knew it.

Some of the men knew Yates, who ran the hardware store. They knew he came from back east somewhere, but so did everyone else. There wasn't a native born in Bodie old enough to lift a mug of beer.

The man Yates had called Deadman snorted. "You trying to decide how to die, Yates? Maybe you'd feel more at home if I turned my back so you could have a good clean shot. You're a coward, Yates, and your fat wife is a whore!"

Yates screamed. His hand darted for his gun in a move that would beat almost anyone in the room. He was fast, he had probably been a gunhand in his day, but the man he called Deadman was faster.

Deadman's left hand whipped downward and the blued six-gun slid out of the holster faster than Spur thought possible. Deadman's right hand brushed back over the metal as his palm cocked the hammer.

Deadman already had the trigger pulled and the hammer fell forward firing the first shot. It caught Yates in the right shoulder and spun him around. Deadman's weapon fired three more times, so quickly it sounded like one long explosion. The last three rounds also hit Yates, one in the chest, one in the throat and the third in the forehead.

His body slammed against the wall, dislodging a southern style whiskey jug where it had hung on a nail. It shattered on the floor. Yates died when the second round hit his heart. He leaned against the wall a moment, a corpse already, then fell to the side and pitched to the Gymnasium floor.

Spur had watched the deadly drama from the end of the bar. He stared at the gunslick and worked the name over in his mind. Deadman . . . Deadman . . . then he had it. Billy Deadman, wanted in most Western states, but few lawmen tried to take him. He often traveled with three partners and was one of the fastest quick draw men in the West.

Spur had never seen him before, but he would remember him now. Blazing fast on the draw and deadly accurate.

Yates had his six gun clear of leather but never got off a shot.

Deadman held his iron on Yates until he was sure he wasn't moving. Then slowly he holstered the .45 Colt and looked around.

"Anybody have any problem with how Yates died? He drew, I drew, it was a fair fight. Now if somebody wants to go get the sheriff or whatever law you have in this town, I'll be right over here at the bar having six straight shots of whiskey."

BODIE BEAUTIES

By the time Billy Deadman walked to the polished counter top at the stand up bar, the apron had poured six shot glasses full of whiskey and lined them up.

Deadman flipped the barkeep a silver dollar and started working on the line of glasses. He stood six feet down the bar from Spur. The two men looked at each other a moment, then Deadman glanced away.

That was when Spur knew the man was a true professional gunman. He used his guns to kill people, not play games.

That was when Spur also knew that before either of them left town, there would be a deadly contest between the two. Spur had no argument with the man, not yet. But he was somehow sure that before he was through in Bodie, this Bodie Badman would be standing across a room or a street from him as both waited to draw.

About five minutes later one of the deputies came in, talked to the barkeep and wrote down his statement, then moved up to Deadman and spoke in hushed tones with him. The chatter in the saloon died out, but still no one could hear what the lawman and the gunman were saying. A moment later the deputy nodded, folded up a small notebook he had been writing in, and walked out the door.

Spur followed him, found the U.S. Hotel and dropped on his bed. It was a lot softer than sleeping under the stars.

Spur got up early the next morning, had breakfast, then walked up to the jail. Captain Trevarow sipped at a cup of coffee in his office. Spur joined him.

"Boys brought in a dead man yesterday. Body dead five or six days. Shot once in the heart, and so

75

close his shirt still showed the powder burns. He's a local named Lenny Abbott. He drifted around. Mine worker for a while, then worked topside, and even did some wood hauling. Nobody seems to know who he worked for last."

"Five days? About the same time as the gold robbery?"

"About. You think there's a connection?"

"Never know. See what else you can find out about him."

"Yeah, we'll do that. I figured just some grudge fight. But there might be a connection."

"What about this Wells Fargo guy, Johnson? Is he honest? He's in a position to know everything. He could grab a shipment, the mine gets paid back by the company, and he winds up with a profit of $25,000."

"Could happen. Has before. But I don't think this time. One of the dead guards on that robbed stage was Johnson's brother-in-law. He wouldn't set up his own kin to be gunned down."

"The killing part could have been by chance. Why would robbers kill everyone on board a stage they cleaned out?"

"Could be any number of reasons."

"But the biggest one is if one of the guards recognized one or more of the robbers. Say I yell out: 'I know you, you're Ingemar Johnson from Bodie' and everyone hears it. Hell, the masked robbers can't just walk away. One or more have been identified, everyone heard the name. The one robber would soon lead to the others. So the robbers must become killers to protect themselves."

"Damn, it probably happened that way. Most robbers out in this neck of the woods don't gun down a whole coach full of folks."

"So this Lenny was a local?"

"Sure, been around two, at least two, three years."

"So lots of people could know him. Even some of the guards might know him—that is, if he was involved in the robbery."

"Possible." Trevarow continued the story. "Say he gets back with the gold, tells his boss how the killings happened, and the top man guns Lenny down to reduce the witnesses and maybe the only contact between the robber/killer and the man who hired them."

"Could happen. Oh, you know that Billy Deadman is in town?"

Trevarow let his chair's front legs drop to the floor. "God, no! Deadeye Deadman? Thought he was still in Kansas."

"Probably got too much warm lead flying around him there. He killed a local last night, an old grudge."

"I heard there was a gun fight, but I haven't read the reports yet. I've never tangled with him, anywhere, never even met the man." Trevarow scowled. "You just be sure you don't kick his spurs. He's a real good man with a six gun."

"I saw him in action last night."

"So?"

"So he's the fastest and the best shot I've ever seen, bar none. Not even you were that fast. So I don't go looking for a stupid gunfight. Never when it's for bragging rights as fastest gun in the state."

"Good. I like having you around town—above ground!"

Spur stood. "Heading down to the Wells Fargo

office. Want them to check on gold shipments."

Ten minutes later, Spur asked Ingemar Johnson his question of the day.

"Has any one mining company been shipping out more gold than it normally does? You can figure the averages for each of the firms and what they're doing now."

"Yes, yes, I see. If one small firm suddenly shipped out an extra $25,000 in gold bullion, it could mean something."

"How better to market stolen gold bullion than to melt it down, recast it in your retort room in your own bullion molds, and then ship it to San Francisco?" Spur asked.

"I get the idea. I'll check the records for the past year, showing the total shipments for each mine for each three month period."

Spur thanked the manager and stepped out of the Wells Fargo office onto Main and turned north. An errant plank in the boardwalk had lost a nail and sprang up two inches. Spur stumbled on it just as a rider on a passing horse fired a six-gun at him from fifteen feet away. Only the stumble saved Spur from serious gunshot damage.

Spur jumped to his feet and glared at the horse and rider who now pounded north on Main. Spur looked along the street, saw a man just stepping down from a horse.

Spur rushed up to him. "I just got shot at, can I borrow your horse?"

Before the man could protest or answer, Spur grabbed the reins, stepped into the saddle and jolted the horse up the street.

"Bring her back!" the owner shouted after him.

Spur waved and kicked the mount in the flanks to

urge her on. The bushwhacker turned off on the next street to the right, which was Union Street. When he saw Spur close behind, he turned left again and rode down a lane in back of the U.S. Hotel to the north, and soon came to Main and pounded past the Bodie Bank and the Moyle warehouse.

Spur's horse was not the fastest, but she seemed to have good staying power. The gunman turned off the street and angled around the old tailing ponds on Bodie creek, then rode into the hills to the north and east of Bodie which was dotted by trailings and overburdens from hundreds of mine tunnels.

The bushwhacker kept moving north, riding along the side of the ridges so his mount didn't have to climb upward. Spur kept chasing him. Now and then the man ahead looked back. He shot twice, but the range was too great.

Once he dodged behind a small mine shack but Spur made a wide turn around it and didn't afford the man an easy shot. He tried, missed, then raced away to the north again.

An hour later they left the last of the mine diggings. They were in open country with only an occasional sagebrush bush showing in the rocky, sandy soil.

Spur guessed they had climbed a thousand feet so were near the 9,500 foot level. There were no trees and no grass up here. The man's horse slowed. For a few paces it limped, then found the gait again.

They came to a flat area and Spur kicked his tired mount into a gallop, closed the distance between them quickly and he fired three fast shots from his six-gun. One of the rounds narrowly missed the bushwhacker, the second sliced through a quarter of an inch of his right shoulder, and the third caught the horse in the head as it turned to look behind.

The horse went down, screaming and kicking in a death struggle.

The gunman rolled behind the horse for some protection and leveled in his six-gun. Spur dropped off his mount and began to stalk his enemy slowly. He moved from one small depression forward, and saw that his target was still behind the horse.

Now he was close enough to call to him.

"Throw out your gun and live," Colt bellowed.

"Go to hell!" the answer came back.

Spur put a round into the horse's dead body.

"Who hired you to try to kill me?" Spur yelled.

"Your wife, you bastard!"

Spur saw a large rock he could use for cover. He fired twice at the bushwhacker, then surged up and ran ten yards to the rock. He felt a hot round of lead slash past him as he dove to safety behind the boulder. Now he had an angle on the gunman. He could see his legs. Spur reloaded his Colt so it held six rounds, then leveled in the weapon across his arm and fired.

A scream of pain billowed from behind the horse.

"Bastard? You shot me!"

"My calling card. Who hired you? Was it the man who held up the stage and killed the guards?"

"Don't know what you're talking about. Jesus, I'm bleeding to death."

"Tell me who hired you and I'll take you down to Doc Rogers."

"Not if I kill you first!"

"You tried and missed. Now it's my turn."

"No!" the man screamed, trailing off the word as he burst from behind the horse, a six-gun in each hand as he charged the rock where Spur lay.

Spur shot him again in the leg and knocked him down. But the gunman staggered up, screamed and charged again, firing with both hands, pinning Spur down. At last Spur pushed around the side of the boulder and fired twice. The bushwhacker was only three feet in front of the rock. The two rounds hit him in the chest and stopped him in his tracks. Slowly his arms dropped to his sides and he turned and fell on the rock.

He was dead.

"Damn!" Spur said. Now he'd never find out who sent the man to gun him down on the street in bright daylight. He went through the man's pockets. He found two new double eagles, probably his blood money. There was a letter from Ohio written to Bobby Hennessy. He had been working at the Standard Mine at one time.

Probably half the men in town had worked the Standard at one time or another. The only other paper was a slip from a laundry with Chinese markings and a bill of sale for a .44 caliber revolver at the price of two dollars and ninety five cents. The gun had been bought that morning.

Spur sat there in the rarified air of the mountain and looked at the dead man. Who was so worried about what Spur McCoy was doing that they hired this man to gun him down? Somebody in town would know the man, know where he worked, who he knew. Spur's one fear was that the man might be a drunk or a down and outer who someone had rescued, sobered him up, bought a gun, given him a horse and pointed out the target.

Two hours later, Spur had walked back to town with Bobby Hennessy draped over the borrowed horse's back. He dropped the body off at Hooperman's undertaking parlor.

Hoop smiled and carried the dead man on his shoulder back to a marble slab in his "work" room.

"More business! I knew you'd be good for business soon as you hit town. You and that Deadman guy could increase my income. Hey, Mr. McCoy, I tell you about the loafer who came by here yesterday? I asked him if he was looking for work. He said not necessarily, but he did want a job."

"Hoop, your jokes are getting worse and worse."

He grinned. "Sorry, McCoy, I guess I'm at a dead end!" He roared with laughter at his own pun and Spur rode back to Main Street and found the man whose horse he had borrowed.

"Any damages to my Princess?" the man asked.

"None at all. She's a fine beast." Spur gave him a silver dollar and walked up to the jail.

Sheriff's Captain Trevarow had some news for him. "We've found out that Lenny Abbott has been in town for four years. He's worked for five different mining companies, including two now out of business and the Standard, the Bodie and Bechtel. That's as far as we are on Lenny."

He eyed Spur. "Heard somebody got shot at on Main Street a couple of hours ago. Was it you?"

"True. I left the bushwhacker's body with Hooperman. Here are his personal effects and papers. His name was Bob Hennessy."

"Hennessy? That one I know. Yeah, had kin in Ohio. A lot like Lenny, he couldn't seem to hold a job for long. I've seen him in saloons lately mooching drinks and finishing off anybody's mug of beer who forgets it for a moment."

"So anybody could have hired him to take a shot at me."

"After they sobered him up, got him a clean shirt, rented him a horse and bought him a gun. According to this receipt, he got the gun today. I'll have a man check to see if the mercantile clerk remembers if anybody was with Bobby when he bought the piece. Then we'll check the livery, too. But chances of finding out who rented the nag for him are slim."

"No way I could keep from killing him. He was on top of me with two guns blasting out hot lead."

"Happens."

"I'm going over to Wells Fargo and see if I can talk Johnson into setting up a fake gold shipment. Nobody will know it's fake except about four of us. We might get lucky."

"Hopefully if you do they won't kill the whole guard force. You gonna sign on Billy Deadman as a guard?"

"Not likely. I'm hoping he rides out of town to a warmer climate since his work is done here."

"Don't count on it. He's still here. Living it up and causing a stir in Virgin Alley. Last night he ordered three girls for all night."

"Damn, nobody's got any secrets in this town— except when they hire a no-good to bushwhack a citizen."

It took Spur a half hour to talk Ingemar Johnson into the fake gold shipment.

"Look, we can put seventy-five pounds of lead in the strong box. Lead is only a little heavier than gold. Nobody needs to know except the bullion man at the mine and the superintendent. All of our people and the guards will think it's a real run. Let's head for Bridgeport this time and see what happens."

Spur set up the coach differently for this trip. He

83

placed quarter-inch iron plates on the inside of the coach to deflect rifle rounds. He removed the panel behind the high driver's seat and took out one of the inside seats so the driver could stand on the floorboards of the coach inside and his head would be high enough so he could look out over the driver's seat and drive. It would give him protection from any first shot, yet still allow him a view of the horses.

To help his view, the cushion that usually is on the high bench was taken off as well. It made a strange looking stage coach, but Spur figured it was worth a try. He tried two drivers before he found one who would drive the coach that way. The man hitched it up and took it on a trial run over some back roads until he was sure he could maneuver the team from such a low position.

Spur made sure all six of the guards inside the coach had Spencer repeating rifles and the sheet iron protected firing positions. There would only be seven men in the coach including the driver and no shotgun guard on the high seat.

The rig rolled out at midnight, stopped at the Bodie mine where Johnson had arranged to pick up seventy-five pounds of pure lead. They charged out the Bridgeport road south and west, and Spur McCoy hoped this would be the night the gold robbers would make another try.

Spur and the guards waited. They rode and watched. The driver cursed. He was getting tired of standing up. The coach rolled past the three best spots for an attack and nothing happened. At four A.M. Spur called the rig to a stop. He explained to the men it had been a dummy run, designed to lure the robbers into another attack, one they wouldn't win.

Spur ordered the stage to turn around and head back for Bodie. One of the men grumbled and was teased because he had what they called 'a bit of poon on the side' in Bridgeport.

The driver asked if he could get back on top where he belonged and Spur said he could.

The men slept the four hour ride back to Bodie. The driver had no one to talk to except the horses and even they got tired of his stories so he began singing to them. At least it kept him awake.

The rig pulled up at the front door of the Wells Fargo office in Bodie about 8 o'clock as any other rig would, only it had dropped off the guards at three places just inside town.

Spur supervised the unloading of the strong box and then went to his hotel to try to finish his half a night's sleep. A letter in his key box caught his attention. By the time he got up to his second story room he had read the note inside.

"Dear Mr. McCoy. I understand you spent some time in New York City. My people are from there. I thought we might have a pleasant chat while dining this day. Could I expect you about one-thirty?" It was signed Mrs. Milly Bechtel. "Oh, my home is at 67 Second Street. Please advise."

Spur went back to the desk, wrote a note, and gave the clerk a quarter to find a boy to deliver it to the widow. Then he went upstairs and fell into his bed and slept four hours. It was half past noon when he woke up. He had an hour.

He shaved, washed up, put on a clean shirt and a pair of trousers, a tie and a jacket. He needed a haircut but that would have to wait. From the room clerk he discovered that Mrs. Bechtel was the widow of the developer of the Bechtel Mine #3. Now she was sole owner and operator. She had a mine superintendent who did most of the day-to-day operation, but she kept her hand on the controls.

"She's what, fat and fifty?" Spur asked.

The clerk laughed. "No indeed. Widow Bechtel is about thirty-five, tall and slender, dresses well and has a fine figure."

Spur thanked him and walked toward the house. At least the time might not be totally wasted. He would get a meal and see a pretty face.

But that wasn't his major problem. He'd tried two dry runs. What did he have to do next to smoke out the robbers? General Halleck back in Washington was probably wondering what he was doing, taking so long to get to a telegraph after his last assignment. Another couple of days here, then he'd have to head for Sacramento with or without the solution of the robbery/massacre.

Ahead he saw an unusual sight in Bodie, a small white house with a picket fence and in the front yard, three blooming rose bushes. Old timers said nothing but hops and sagebrush would grow in Bodie because of the severe winters.

Spur paused to admire the roses. All three bushes were in five gallon buckets. He guessed the owner of them took them inside the house during the winter season.

A woman in her thirties came around the corner, saw him and smiled. "I hope you're enjoying my rose garden," she said. "These are the only roses in all of Bodie."

"Beautiful, ma'am, simply beautiful. Oh, could I buy one of the red blooms?"

"I usually don't pick them. They last so much longer on the bush."

"I'm going to see a lady for dinner, and I thought a rose might be a welcome gift."

"A lady, well. Certainly. How can I stand in the way of a gentleman and a lady." She snipped a red bloom with a foot long stem, trimmed off the thorns and all but two leaves and handed it to him.

"My compliments to you and to the lady. I'm sure she'll know where it came from."

"I thank you, you're most kind. What was your name?"

"Mrs. Wilson. Mrs. Emma Wilson. Enjoy."

Spur found the Bechtel house, a grand three story affair with a bay window, and a porch along the length of the house in the grand style. It was by far the most lavish house he had seen in Bodie. Most houses here were square boxes with low ceilings so they would be easier to heat, more utilitarian than fancy.

At the front door, he lifted a brass knocker and let it fall against a heavy brass plate.

A small, delicate, beautiful Chinese girl opened the door, smiled shyly and motioned for him to follow. They went through a small hallway, then into a parlor that was grand. It reminded him of one of his father's houses in New York. Warm toned wood dominated the room in the furniture, in a wall panel, and around a massive stone fireplace.

On the walls hung three oil paintings that were bold and colorful and of excellent quality.

At a small table ready for two near a bay window, sat a red headed woman who watched him with interest.

"Good afternoon, Mr. McCoy. I'm Milly Bechtel. It's good to meet you after hearing so many good things about you. I feel I must be the social leader in town, so welcome to Bodie."

Up close her skin was flawless, a soft not quite pinkish white to go with her hair color. Her wide set eyes were of the palest green and the red/green combination made him think of a Christmas tree. A delicate nose commanded a well formed mouth that showed just a touch of self applied color.

"I hope I pass approval," she said with a smile.

"I'm sorry, how rude of me. But it isn't often I find amazingly beautiful women in Bodie. Thank you for inviting me. The hotel food is becoming quite the same."

"My pleasure to have you come, especially since you have said nice things and brought me a rose. It must have come from Emma Wilson's garden. She's a marvel with flowers."

Spur handed the rose to her. She sniffed it delicately, then gave it to the small Chinese girl who placed it in a bone china vase and set it on the table.

"Now, our table is complete! I miss the vases and vases filled with flowers that I always used to have on occasions like this."

They began the meal with a robust white wine, then had diamond shaped sandwiches made of some sturdy brown bread, buttered with mayonnaise and stuffed with the best marinated roast quail meat he had ever tasted.

"Would I be impolite if I asked for another of those delicious sandwiches?" Spur asked.

At once the Chinese girl brought him two.

"I love watching a man enjoy a meal," Mrs. Bechtel said. "Now tell me about yourself. Somebody said you were a college man."

Spur laughed. "I haven't heard that term since I left New York. In most of the country it has little meaning. Yes, I grew up in New York City, then went to Harvard for my degree in business."

"How marvelous! I attended a small woman's

college for one year, then I married Harry . . . eventually I wound up here in the gold mining business.''

"That's very brave of you. This is such a male dominated business.''

"I am good at knowing who to hire. I find the best men to do the job, pay them more than anyone else, and make money. That seems to be what everyone is trying to do. Even when the wood supply gets short toward the end of winter, the wood sellers raise the price as high as thirty dollars a cord. Usually, it costs eight to ten dollars in the summer and fall. Now that is what I call good business!''

She watched him a moment.

"Tell me more about what you do. I'm always on the watch for good people. Maybe I could hire you, with your business degree and all.''

Spur laughed. "No, I'm afraid not. I know nothing about the mining business. I'm in town to visit an old friend, Captain Trevarow. Haven't seen him in four or five years, so we have a lot of catching up to do.''

"So we should have a social occasion in your honor, a party or a dance, something.''

"I'm not good at parties, Mrs. Bechtel, but thank you for the thought. I was here five years ago, and the growth of the town has been tremendous. Just how big do you think Bodie can get?''

"Gracious, I have no idea. I'd say it may be somewhere near the peak. We haven't had a really good new strike in any of the mines now for six months. The top of the boom may be coming soon. Once that happens it's all down hill with the scrappy ones hanging on until the last seam of gold has been dug out.''

"All good things come to an end," Spur said.

"I've lived in three mining towns. One of them little more than a tent city that never reached the wooden building stage. I know about empty dreams."

The Chinese girl came in and cleared away the things. She watched Spur every moment she was there, he noticed.

"Me Ling is such a good helper. She's fascinated by you. She speaks only Chinese."

"She's beautiful."

The girl sensed their talking about her and took the last of the lunch things and left.

"May I play the piano for you? It's one of my treasures. I had it shipped out here by boat and wagon. A piano tuner worked on it for two weeks to get it back in condition to play."

"I'd enjoy hearing you play, Mrs. Bechtel, but I do have an appointment I must keep in about fifteen minutes. I've enjoyed the meal, and the fine company. This room is outstanding. It looks something like one that was my mother's favorite in our Park Avenue house. Truly amazing."

He stood. "Thank you again for a wonderful time. Perhaps I can hear you play another time soon. I'm sorry, but I really do need to go now."

"I understand. Business, even though you're here on a friendly visit. Perhaps sometime in the evening would be better for you. I'll be in touch with you, Mr. McCoy."

She walked him to the door. He kissed her hand as he left, and she seemed about to say something, then stopped.

Spur hurried down the walk to the street. There had to be a way to rout out the killers. It was his job to figure it out. He headed back to the jail, hoping that by now the sheriff's deputies had found something about the dead bushwhacker that would tie him in with the killers.

6

Sheriff's Captain Trevarow shook his head. "Sorry, McCoy. That's all we can find out. A tall man with a fake red beard and heavy glasses bought the gun with Hennessy early this morning. The same man rented a horse at Kirkwood Stables an hour later. Then the red bearded man vanished.

"Oh, Kirkwood wants you to pay him twenty dollars for the horse you shot. I took it out of the forty dollars you found on Hennessy's body, so you're off the cowcatcher on that one."

"This outfit sure covered its tracks. They knew if something went wrong we'd check back on Hennessy. Dammit, John. We're right back where we started."

"Maybe not, Spur. A man who claimed Lenny's body said far as he knew, Lenny still worked at the Bechtel Mining Company as of last Friday when he disappeared."

"Bechtel. Doesn't mean a thing. I just had dinner

with the owner of that mine. Seemed like a right respectable lady."

John grinned. "Figured Milly might be making time with you. She's been something of a spicy item since her husband died. All very proper, of course. A lot of woman, that Milly."

"So what the hell are we supposed to do now?" Spur asked, his impatience beginning to show.

John chuckled. "How long you been at this law work, McCoy? You know what to do, we sit and wait, keep our eyes open, and hope that the killers make a mistake."

"This isn't a bank robbery, John. The killers can't spend gold bullion."

"But the actual holdup men must have been paid in cold cash. Where are the big spenders? I haven't heard of any lately around this town."

"Maybe they rode on to Bridgeport. Why come back here?"

"Unless this was where the boss was, and where they had to deliver the gold."

"If Lenny was one of the gang, he sure isn't going to spend much. You've talked to the girls up in the fancy lady houses?" Spur asked.

"Yep. First thing. Things seem to be more quiet than usual up there. Don't ask me why."

"I'm no good at waiting, John. Never have been. Think I'll go get a beer." He stopped. "What about Chinatown? Anybody up there be of any help? Sometimes they see things we don't."

"I don't talk Chink too good. Most of them don't speak any English at all. My best contact is Chou. He's a kind of head boss up there. I've got everyone listening."

"Good, time I did some serious drinking."

"Got a later engagement with the widow Milly?"

Trevarow asked.

"No. If I did, I wouldn't share all that woman with you anyway. Go find your own girl." Spur grinned as he stalked out of the office and back up King Street to Main.

Six, two-mule wagons went by loaded down with tightly packed four foot cordwood. From the looks of it the wood was all split pine. A sign on the side of the last load offered the wood for sale to the first customer for $12 a cord.

As Spur looked around the community he now noticed that cord wood in four feet lengths was stacked everywhere. In back of the Standard Stamp Mill he had seen a huge pile of neatly stacked and split cord wood that was a hundred feet long, twenty feet wide and eight feet high.

August was the time to be laying in the winter's wood supply for certain. An item in the Bodie Weekly Standard newspaper said there were now over 19,000 cord of wood in the Bodie community and half again that much would be needed before the snow closed the roads to all except freight sleighs.

Spur followed the last wagon and saw it pull in at a vacant lot across from the U.S. Hotel. The lot was jammed on the far end with stacked cord wood. A short man with a derby hat sat in a chair next to a small shack as he talked to a man and his wife. They argued for a moment, then the man produced eleven dollars and gave it to the salesman.

Spur walked up on the end of the sale.

"Right, Mr. Vernon. Have it at your place within the hour. Yep, I know the house. You be there to tell the driver where to put it. We don't stack, just throw it off. Right." The couple went down the street and Spur moved up to the small man.

"Business looks good," Spur said.

The man stood but was still only five feet tall. He held out a soft, pink hand.

"Indeed it is, stranger. My name is Zentner, Stump Zentner, in case you need to know. Need some good pine cordwood? I can cut that twelve dollar price a bit."

"Sorry, can't use any. I don't own a stove."

Stump scowled. "You're gonna freeze your balls off before Spring." He frowned. "You funnin' me, right? We got Hoop to make all the bad jokes we need in town. You really don't have a stove?"

"Be moving on long before snow time, Mr. Zentner. I've never seen so much firewood in my life."

"Fiddlefoot, huh? Okay, by me. Mills and steam lifts are what use most of the wood. I used to have a contract with the Bodie, but some jackass cut the rate to seven dollars a cord and I wouldn't meet his price. Course they buy two, three hundred cord at a time. Makes a man plumb tired just thinking about all that axe, saw and sledge work."

Spur waved and moved on up the street. He hadn't been to the Chinese district yet. Spur retraced his steps past the jail on King Street and into the Chinese houses and a few shops. They seemed self sufficient. He knew there were a few Chinese laundries in town but he wasn't sure what the rest of the people did.

These must be the workers and their descendents who came to the country to help build the transcontinental railroad that was completed back in 1869. Over ten years ago. Spur received some angry glances and after a block or two he turned and walked out of the district.

It seemed like a whole new world in there, and not one that he really needed to enter at the moment.

As he left he saw a miner moving in that direction. He seemed to be drunk, but hardly staggered. Spur thought of warning him, but the man had been there longer than Spur. The Secret Service agent watched him for a while. He wore a full set of whiskers that were now half white and half black and four inches long. He probably could take care of himself. Spur went back to Main Street to see what he could dig up about the killers. Somebody had to know something.

The miner Spur saw continued up King Street, turned off in a narrow lane between closely bunched shacks and houses until he saw what he wanted, a young Chinese girl who rushed from one building to another.

She wasn't fast enough. The miner moved quickly, cut off the girl's escape and grabbed her by one arm. He spun her around and pushed her against an unpainted building.

"Yeah, Chink poon on the hoof! Damn, I'm gonna find out for sure if this Chink stuff is cut sideways. Everybody says so." He laughed, pulled the girl close to him and whispered something in her ear.

She chattered at him in Chinese, then she screamed. The miner slapped her hard, bouncing her head to one side.

"Shut up, Chink-O. Quiet time. My name is Big Al and I don't take no shit off nobody, specially some stick thin Chink poontah like you."

In one swift move he grabbed the light fabric of her blouse front and jerked downward. Seams parted and fabric ripped and her blouse and thin chemise ripped to her waist exposing her small breasts.

"Yeah, least ways these Chink poon got tits," the miner yelped. He pushed up against her now, his hips grinding hard at hers. She screamed again, and three Chinese men appeared in a doorway behind them. The miner spun around, drew a knife from his boot and waved it at them.

"Just back off, Chink-heads. None of your goddamned business. Back off!" He waved the knife again and they moved into the doorway.

Big Al turned, pushed the knife back in his boot and rubbed her breasts. Then he tried to open the buttons on his fly. With just one hand he had trouble. The girl screamed again and clawed fingernails down his cheek leaving red scratches that started to bleed through his beard.

"Fucking Chink whore!" the miner screeched. He slapped her. She jerked away from him and ran but he caught her quickly. Two Chinese men jumped from another doorway in front of the girl. Both had foot long knives and they advanced on the miner. Big Al held the girl in front of him now, his arm tightly around her stomach holding her as a shield.

"Get out of here, dirty Chinks! You got no cause to get messed in this."

The two men advanced, their deadly knives ready.

"You come a step more and I'm gonna slit this pretty poon's throat. Now you don't want me to have to do something like that, do you boys."

They made no indication that they understood. Now they moved apart and came at him from angles, cutting off any escape.

"Goddamn, you boys don't believe me."

Big Al swept the sharp blade across the girl's throat, then pushed her at one of the men making him stumble. The miner charged the second one, took a cut on his arm, but drove his blade into the man's upper chest.

By then two more Chinese men jumped out from

doorways behind him. One darted in and before the miner knew they were behind him, the man struck him on the back of the head with a four foot long staff. Big Al went down and unconscious on the ground.

When the miner woke up he stood in a building with three lamps lighting it. It was dark outside and around him he heard nothing but Chinese talking with each other. A glass of water had been sloshed in his face and he came fully awake and realized he was naked and standing with his hands above his head where they were tied to a cross rafter on the open ceiling.

"What the hell?" he shouted. An inch-thick staff thudded into his left kidney and Big Al bawled in agony. He vomited and just as he recovered, someone hit him in the other kidney.

When he could look up, Big Al saw the Chinese man he had stabbed in the shoulder come up and hold a long thin knife for Big Al to see.

Chou said something to the man, showed him the knife again, then pointed at his bandaged shoulder.

"Yeah, so I stuck you. Little bastard, you asked for it."

Chou shook his head, put the knife carefully on Big Al's arm and drew a six inch line as blood flowed. The cut wasn't deep, perhaps a quarter of an inch, but blood filled the wound and spilled down his arm.

Big Al screamed and tried to kick the Chinaman, but his ankles had been tied together.

"Bastard!" the miner roared.

Chou made a slight bow to Big Al and handed the blade to another Chinese who stood behind him. The man spat in Big Al's face, then made a cut, this time on his cheek. Blood flowed and dripped off his beard.

Big Al screamed again.

The Chinese man bowed and handed the blade to the next man in line. For a moment Big Al looked at the line of Chinese that stretched to the back of the room. He screamed.

Someone slapped his face. He looked at the man who stood there.

"My name is Chou. I am protector of my people in this small city. We retain our customs. Today you killed a niece of mine, a fine young girl. Now you will suffer your punishment. May your god forgive you and your soul rest in peace."

"What the hell? I don't go by no damned Chink law."

The knife made its ritual slice on his body and more blood appeared.

"Get me out of here, Chou! Go get the Captain, Trevarow. Damnit, Chou, I ain't no damn Chink!"

A small woman next in line reached up and slapped him in the face. She screamed at him a dozen words, them made a foot long slice across his stomach and watched in satisfaction as the blood puddled along the slash and ran down into his pubic hair.

When she left, Chou spoke again. "That was the dead girl's mother. She wanted to slice off your penis. I told her no. She asked our god to burn your feet in hell for a thousand years and to move the fire up your body an inch every thousand years after that."

Big Al Grogotsky looked at the line of Chinese and felt the knife slice into his flesh again, and he was morning-after sober. He realized for the first time that he was in deep trouble and this was one jam he might not live through.

* * *

The next morning Spur stopped at the Sheriff's office. He was on his way to see Jessica who had sent him a note that said she had someone who wanted to meet him at ten that morning at the house just off Bonanza.

Captain Trevarow motioned Spur to follow him and they went down Bonanza a ways to the undertaker. A man had been laid out on the marble slab in the back room. He was naked, but it was hard to tell. His entire body was marked with hundreds of individual knife cuts. There were angry slashes through his four-inch beard, but none across his throat.

"That's the hard way to die," McCoy said, looking at the body. "The man suffered more than any human being should have to."

"Never seen that before," Trevarow said. "Heard about it, being around the Chinese."

"The death of a thousand slashes," Spur said. "The Chinese reserve it as a method of execution for the most terrible of crimes against their people. This guy with the beard could be the one I saw walking into that area yesterday. Any idea what happened?"

"Not a clue, and I never will know. I let the Chinese take care of things in their little village. Chou is the head man up there now and he does a good job."

"Something like this means the man killed somebody, more likely somebody young who would have had a long life to look forward to."

Hooperman came up wiping his hands on a towel. "Maybe the slob died before they were through carving him," the undertaker said.

"Not a chance. The idea is not to kill him, just make him suffer. All of those wounds have bled. That means his heart was still pumping. The worst cut won't bleed once the pump stops. No reason blood should run out when there's no pressure in the pipe."

Hoop made a deep bow to Spur. "The man is a poet, a scholar. I'd give a cheer if this wasn't such a *grave* moment." Hooperman held his sides as he roared laughing.

"Eventually, the victim dies of loss of blood," Spur said. "Of course, that could take half the night."

"He's been dead about four hours," Hoop said, lifting one hand and letting it drop. It went back to the slab slowly as rigormortis worked its way into the flesh.

Spur and Trevarow walked back to the jail.

"Nothing to get the morning started off right like a nice fresh body," Spur said. "You want a blood red steak for breakfast?"

Trevarow took a swing at him but missed.

"Anything more on your two dead suspects?"

"Not a word."

"I got a note from one of the fancy house girls this morning. Might prove to be a lead."

"Can't tell till you ask," Trevarow said.

Spur found the right house, went up to the door and started to knock, but a sign said: "Come on in!"

He knocked and then went inside. A floozy in a robe hurried out of sight. Spur rang a small dinner bell on a stand up desk at the side of the room.

Jessica hurried in through a draped door.

"You're early as usual, Spur McCoy. Around here nobody gets up until noon. Hetti wants to meet you. She said ten, but ten-thirty will be better. I heard about the slice job last night. That gives me the shivers."

"You don't have to worry about the Chinese.

BODIE BEAUTIES

None of them will bother you, if you don't hurt them. My guess is that some drunken miner killed somebody in Chinatown last night, and they served justice in their own way, a life for a life."

"I still shiver." She stopped, reached up and kissed him gently on the lips. "Now, let me tell you why I asked you to come. First, I want you to meet Hetti. She's a dear, the best lady I've ever worked for.

"Hetti is a prim and proper lady from Boston. The gossip is that she's still a virgin at sixty-two, but I couldn't say. She demands absolute ladylike behavior of her girls until they get behind closed doors. In the parlor we are fully clothed, we all carry fans, our hair is fixed nicely, and we wear just a little makeup, not all painted like the dance hall girls. She calls us a quality product. We can't use bad language either. We have to take a bath twice a day and we can't use too much perfume."

"Even now you smell good," Spur said.

"Good. Hetti also demands absolute gentlemanly conduct from our customers. No weapons are permitted in the rooms. They have to check six-guns, knives and hideouts in the lobby. If a girl finds a weapon on a man she throws it out the window.

"Any man gets out of line we have two huge black men who come in and pitch them out into the street. Once last month a guy got belligerent, a mean drunk, I guess. He slapped Wanda and she screamed for the boys. These two blacks, who stand about six-feet-six each and weigh about 285 pounds, rushed into her room, carried the drunk out, and sat him down on the porch. He swore at them and slugged one. Then they took his pistol and knife, picked him up, carried him to the street and threw

103

him into the dust. They dumped the rounds out of his six-gun and threw it down the street. About a dozen people were on hand to laugh at him.

"Well, like I said, Hetti is about sixty, rich some say, and she charges twice as much as any other house on the street. That makes us feel kind of special."

She squeezed Spur's hand. "I'm just so glad to see you. I'll never forget what you did for me in Salt Lake."

Jessica fluffed out her long blonde hair and smiled. "McCoy, I head something the other night and Miss Hetti said I have to tell somebody. Usually we don't, but this is too important, she said."

Jessica looked at a Seth Thomas on the wall, and stood. "Let's go see her."

They went down a hall and to a fancy door. Jessica knocked and a few moments later it opened. A tiny woman of about sixty stood there in a dignified, expensive dress. Her hair was pure white and carefully set on top of her head. A diamond necklace showed around her throat and she smiled and waved them inside with a hand that had three rings.

"Yes, the government man, please come in."

Spur looked at her trying to remember. At last he smiled and nodded. They sat down on expensive upholstered furniture in a bit of an old fashioned parlor, and Spur smiled. "It's good to see you, Lotti," he said.

Jessica looked at him in surprise.

"Yes, McCoy. I wondered when you were going to remember. You couldn't have been much over twenty at the time."

"Twenty-one, and my first trip to New Orleans."

"Jessica, dear, you are not hearing any of this."

"No, ma'am."

"Neither am I, Hetti. Jessica said she heard something important. I'm really stumped on this one. I've got no leads, nowhere to go, and ten dead men glaring at me in my sleep."

"Charles, we might be able to help. The important parts, Jessica."

"This guy was celebrating, an all nighter. He was more than a little drunk on champagne. He gave me a twenty dollar tip at the start of the night. Then he got to talking. He was a big talker. Bragged about all the rotten, illegal things he'd done. Most of them were out of the state. He said that wasn't nothing. Just his practice, his training ground.

"Then later he asked me if I'd ever seen anything worth twenty-five thousand dollars. I said all the time, my diamonds and jewels. I just put it down to drunk talk.

"He mentioned the same figure two or three times, and then I remembered the Bodie Standard talked about that was how much the stolen gold shipment was worth."

"Tell Spur what you did then, Jess."

Jessica walked to the window and looked out through the heavy drapes, then came back. "I know we're not supposed to, Hetti, but I deliberately got him talking about the money again. Pretty soon he admitted he didn't have the money, but he did own that much gold, for a few hours. That much gold in his possession, he said, gave him a feeling he'd never had before."

"Did he say what he did with it, where it went, what happened, anything else about the gold?"

"No, he got so drunk he passed out and I couldn't wake him until morning. He just slept off all the champagne."

"We know who the man is, Spur," Hetti said. "I felt that with those eight murders, we didn't have to worry about our rule of client confidentiality."

"I'm glad. Who's the man?"

Jessica looked over at Hetti who nodded.

"His name is Eli Johl," Jessica said. "He's the mine superintendent and manager at the Bechtel Mine #3."

Spur whistled. "Yeah, yeah! We may be getting somewhere."

"This helped?"

"It's a start. Before, we had nothing."

"The Bechtel is owned by the widow of the founder," Hetti said. "I've heard that it isn't doing all that well."

Jessica nodded.

"Yes, Jess, you run along. Send in some of that good wine and those little crackers we like."

When Jessica left Spur took her hand. "I knew Jessica in Salt Lake a few years ago."

"She told me about it. You can do no wrong in her eyes. Mine either. Where have the years gone?"

"You used them well. Jessica says the girls would die for you, that you run the best house in town and that you protect them like jewels."

"They are jewels, my jewels."

A small Chinese woman brought in a bottle of wine and two glasses and a moonstone dish filled with small cheese flavored crackers.

"You may do the wine," Hetti said.

Spur uncorked the bottle and poured. The crackers were good.

Hetti smiled as she watched Spur. "You're just as intense now as you were then," she said. "A government man. I know you're itching to get back on the case. I know, I know."

"First, a toast to the good old days."

"I can drink to that."

The wine was tangy, robust. Spur drained his glass and reached for Hetti's hand. "Thanks for the help. It may get us moving down the right road. Take care of Jessica."

Jessica was waiting outside the door to lead him out of the house. All was still quiet as the working girls slept in. At the door Jessica kissed his cheek. "I want to see you again before you leave. I'll get another night off."

"Soon," Spur said. "You've really helped a lot." He tipped up her chin and kissed her lips, then turned and hurried down the steps. He had an entirely new slant on the case.

The manager of the Bechtel would certainly have the whole facility of the mine and the retort room available for his uses. Say he did arrange the robbery, one of the guards identified one of the robbers and they had to be killed.

It was possible that Lenny drew the wrath of Elí and he was wiped out. Maybe that left no connection between the robbery and Bechtel? That was what he had to work on.

7

Spur stepped into the Wells Fargo office, waved at the people there who knew him by now and walked back to the manager's office. Johnson was in.

Spur sat in a chair beside the desk, took a cup of coffee from Ingemar and sipped at it.

"So? Have you caught my robbers yet?"

"Working on it, Mr. Johnson. Just wondered if the Bechtel Mine has a gold shipment scheduled for sometime soon."

Johnson looked up quickly, a questioning frown on his face.

"Matter of fact . . ." he stopped. "The Bechtel hasn't been doing all that well. They ship out maybe a hundred and fifty thousand a year. That's not a whole lot of trips. Why would you wonder if they might have a shipment about now?"

"Just a guess. Did you average out those gold shipments like we talked about?"

"Did. So far it looks like everybody is on

schedule." He looked down a list. "Except . . . except the Bechtel. If they are working the same vein at the same level, they should have another shipment of twenty to twenty-five thousand ready the end of next month."

"But they've set one for tomorrow night?"

"Yes. Another guess?"

"No, you looked so upset I figured it had to be. Bechtel isn't due yet. Where do you suppose they got the new gold bullion?"

"Not for me to say," Johnson stammered. "Look, I've shown you more of our company records now than . . ."

"Relax, Johnson. What we're doing here is trying to run down some killers and some gold robbers, and save your firm twenty-five thousand dollars. You've got to help. I need a copy of those figures for Bechtel's shipments for the past two years."

Johnson looked out his window, then nodded. "Damn, I guess it won't hurt. If it will help . . ."

"It will. I want that same rig we used before and the same driver if he's available. We'll keep him inside the rig. Be my guess that tomorrow night won't be a dry run for us. Say Bechtel is somehow behind the gold heist, why not steal their own shipment and multiply their profits?"

"Yes, it makes sense when we talk about it. But Milly Bechtel?"

"Nobody says the widow has to be involved. One of Hetti's girls had a big-spending, big-drinking, big-talking customer the other night. He kept chatting about how beautiful twenty-five thousand dollars in gold was. We know who he is, and think we have a real good lead. It all might pay off tomorrow night."

Johnson nodded. "The same driver is in town. I'll

schedule him and six guards and you, like that fake run. We'll leave at ten P.M. heading for Carson City through Aurora."

"Good enough, Ingemar. This time I want the gold to be stolen. We'll instruct the guards not to resist too strenuously. We make them think we're defending it all out, but let them win without getting anybody killed."

"I don't understand. Why let them steal more gold?"

"I won't be on the stage. I'll have a team of six deputy sheriffs riding behind the gold wagon, back far enough to be out of sight. As soon as the gold wagon is hit, we'll ride up to make sure that the robbers aren't killing anyone. Then when the heist is over, we'll follow the gold robbers and see where they go, find out the boss, nab him and the stolen gold, and solve the whole thing."

"Is that possible?" Ingemar asked. "A lot of things could go wrong and we'd lose more gold."

"Might happen, but not with good planning, and good men. You put in seven guards and the driver, and keep him inside the rig. Then the only thing that can get killed is a lead horse."

Ingemar hit his coffee which probably was whiskey laced again. Spur watched him. His nerves were shredding.

"You really . . . you really think it'll work?"

"I do, and I think the robbers will know when we're leaving and which route we take, before we go. I'm not sure how they do that."

"Let's try it. If I don't get that twenty-five thousand back, I'm going to be fired anyway. They can only fire me once for losing two gold shipments."

"Sounds good to me, Mr. Johnson. I'll meet you at

the Bechtel Mine #3 with the deputies."

Spur walked back to Main Street feeling better than he had in a week. He went to see John Trevarow and explained to him about the talk with Hetti and then with Johnson.

"Looks like you've got a good loop on these varmints, McCoy," the Sheriff's Captain said.

"Not yet. We've got some tracks. You assign me six deputies who can ride well for tomorrow night and we'll have a better handle. Then I want to put three or four men in a line outside of town about a mile in case they get away from us."

"No problem there, Spur."

"Good. This time we have a real shot at them, because I think they'll hit the stage. But we haven't got the gold or the culprits yet. Even if they do come from Bechtel it could be any one of fifty people."

"Could, but probably ain't."

"Gold bullion. As I understand it, each mine pours the molten gold into forms and each mine has its name in the form, right?"

"True. On top of the bullion bar it will read STD Bodie, for the Standard; BODIE Bodie for the Bodie; BECHT Bodie for Bechtel; and so on."

"So one mine can't sell another mine's bullion."

"Not unless they remelt it and recast it in the retort room using their own molds."

"I heard once that a chemical analysis of gold could pinpoint where it came from, which mine, which vein. Is that true?"

"Might be. Virginia City gold would be different than ours. But I'm not so sure that gold mined from one end of this vein would be different than gold mined from the other end of it."

"So I'll make a big bluff when I have to," Spur said. "If it gets down to that fine a line."

Spur left the jail and headed toward his hotel. He saw Captain Trevarow come out behind him and stand in the sun a moment. That was when a gunshot sounded and the Captain's hat spun off his head. Two men came across the street and stopped thirty feet away from the lawman.

"Hear you're an old time gunsharp, Captain," one of the men called. "Hear you're about the fastest thing in town. We've come to find out just how fast you really are."

Spur had turned as soon as he heard the shot and now walked back to the jail and stepped up beside the lawman.

"Afternoon, gents. Thought this party needed a little bit of evening up."

"We didn't invite nobody else," the taller one said.

"Invited myself, and I got forty-five good reasons why I should stay, right here on my hip. You objecting?"

"The big gunman don't have his pistola with him," the other gunman said. He stood loose, hand near his weapon, knees slightly bent. Spur knew he would be the fastest.

"Duffy!" Trevarow called. "Bring me out my gunbelt!"

A deputy ran out of the jail a moment later with the leather and Trevarow strapped it on.

"Boys, you don't have to do this," Sheriff Deputy Travarow said. "It's an even match now. You want to, you just keep your hands away from iron and walk up to Main Street and have a drink. No reason anybody needs to die here today."

"Hey, I'm not worried about it. You, old man, you're the one who should be worried. Figure I take you out, and then your friend here who butts into

113

other folks' business. Then I find that other guy in town, what's his name? Deadman, Billy Deadman. I hear he can shoot a bit."

Spur relaxed, moved a foot or so more away from Trevarow, then watched the two gunmen thirty feet away. He had no idea how good either one was. The short one first.

"Any time you're ready . . . " Before Spur could finish, the visitors went for their weapons.

Spur's draw was smooth, liquid fast. He caught the butt, lifted the weapon, dragged back the hammer and when the muzzle slanted up he put his first round through the shorter man's chest, blasting him backward. The tall one was slower, his gun still coming out when Spur saw Trevarow fighting to get his weapon out of leather.

Spur timed it and just as Trevarow's gun muzzle was coming up, Spur fired again, the bullet blasting into the tall man's belly, punching him sideways into the dust, his gun jolting three feet from his hand..

Spur and John Trevarow moved forward checking the gunmen. The short one was dead. The tall one swore softly.

"Sombitch! Nobody is that fast. I had the old man dead to rights! Nobody is that fast." He screamed, doubled over and blood came pouring out of his mouth. Then he bellowed in pain and the sound died as a final gush of air whispered out of his dead lungs.

Three men ran up. They looked at the dead men, then at the lawman.

"You gave them every chance, Captain," one of the men said. "You told them to walk away."

"But I didn't . . . "

"You did what you had to do, Sheriff. That should discourage some of the other young savages in town who think they can draw a .45 on you!"

Captain Trevarow looked hard at Spur. At last he nodded. "Yep. Deed it should discourage them."

There were thanks in his eyes. He pointed to two men. "Get these bodies down to Hooperman. Ain't a far walk from here. Can't have this sort of thing littering our streets."

More men arrived, and a sprinkling of women. The bodies were carried away and Spur and Trevarow went back into the jail.

"John, I didn't even notice that you didn't have on your guns."

"No matter." He waved toward his office and the men went in and closed the door.

"That's absolutely the last time I try to fast draw," Trevarow said. "You saw what happened. If you hadn't picked the fastest gun to take out first, I'd be on that marble slab right now. The tall one was slow as sin and still he beat me. Leastwise I got my muzzle up before you killed the second one. Thanks for waiting so it looked like I shot him."

"When are these young gunsharps going to give up and let a man stay retired?"

"Hell, McCoy, you know the answer to that. Probably never, at least as long as the six-gun is important in the West. Maybe about the turn of the century things will ease off a little. I won't be around to see that day."

"Might surprise yourself. That's only twenty-one more years. You'll hit eighty at least before we stuff your boots upside down on somebody's fence posts."

"Damn well hope so." Trevarow sat down, took off his hat and wiped sweat off his forehead. "Christ, I thought I was dead out there. Would have been if it hadn't . . ."

Spur held up his hand. "You're still wearing your iron."

Trevarow stood and took off the belt, checked the five loads still in the cylinder and hung it on a nail in the wall.

"Hope to hell I can leave that thing over there."

"I'm betting that you can," Spur said.

Captain Trevarow began writing out the paper work on the two dead men and Spur headed down to his hotel where he had been going before.

At the desk the clerk gave him an envelope along with his key. Upstairs in his room he read the note. It was from Mrs. Bechtel:

"Mr. McCoy. We never did get around to talking about New York when you were here. Could I possibly persuade you to have supper with me tonight, about seven? I hope so. We have so much to talk about and people from New York so seldom come into a small town like this. I look forward to seeing you tonight for supper. If for any reason you can't come, send me a note."

It was signed Milly Bechtel. He noticed the absence of the Mrs. on the name. It probably meant nothing. On the other hand, a nice quiet supper with their prime suspect mine owner couldn't hurt a thing. He might do a little questioning, on a relaxed basis, of course.

Spur changed jackets to one of well worn jeans material, had a sandwich and a cup of coffee at the Laurel Palace Chop Stand, and meandered along the boardwalk down Main trying to reason out any new angle on the gold robbery. The Bechtel seemed to be the prime suspect. Every clue so far pointed that way, but how could he be sure?

Ride the gold wagon and hope it was hit was the best plan. They could surrender, make sure the guards weren't killed and then follow the culprits. That would take two forces, one on the coach, one following at a safe distance. Just the way he had set it up. He hoped it would work.

Spur ambled down one side of Main and up the other. Scattered among the sixty-five saloons were three times that many other businesses. There was about anything now in Bodie that a man could want, from garters to goiter medicine.

Doc Rogers had help now with three more doctors in town and even a dentist or two. Mr. Nobel at the Standard Market was showing an interesting variety of fresh fruits from Sonora and Sacramento. There were apples, pears, bananas, apricots and strawberries in season.

Spur stopped at the San Francisco Market on Main. Peaches were twenty cents a pound. He bought two and ate them as he walked. The market also had fresh vegetables of most kinds, even tomatoes at fifteen cents a pound. He paid a dollar for a nice watermelon and figured he'd take it with him as an offering to the widow Bechtel.

At the newspaper office he saw an advertisement from Aurora in the Bodie Standard that the Exchange Market had beef at six cents a pound when bought by the quarter.

On the other hand, milk was scarcer in Bodie because there was little graze for the cattle. Mr. Huntoon advertised that he'd deliver milk for fifty cents a quart.

Spur leaned against the newspaper office front wall for a minute to soak up some sun. Even in August Bodie had its chilly moments during the day. At last he figured out it was the wind which seemed in a rush to get across the 8,500 foot level of the mountains and on to the east. He had no idea where it was going.

He could come up with no other prospect than the Bechtel people. Who would have the retort room available to melt down and recast the gold? The manager, maybe a foreman. Now it was wait and see.

That evening at just before seven, he arrived at the widow Bechtel's mansion in a sparkling clean shirt and jacket, tie and clean trousers. Even his boots were shined.

The small Chinese girl opened the door, smiled, and led him into the parlor. Mrs. Bechtel sat playing the piano. She knew several of the old Civil War songs.

"Mr. McCoy. Right on time. So nice that you could come. I try to play a little every day so I don't lose my skills, such as they are."

She moved from the piano bench to the upholstered couch and waved him into a matching chair.

A moment later the Chinese girl, Me Ling, came in with drinks on a silver serving tray.

"A little branch water and whiskey will set up our dinner nicely, Mr. McCoy."

They lifted off the glasses and she raised hers in a toast. "To your good health, Mr. McCoy, and may all of your enterprises be profitable."

"I'll drink to that. You sound like you're becoming a real businesswoman, Mrs. Bechtel."

"I'm trying. How is your business in town progressing?"

"Slowly, I'm afraid. I had thought of buying into one of the mines while I was here, but nothing seems available right now—at least nothing that seems worthwhile."

"Empty holes are cheap in Bodie," she said.

Spur sipped his whiskey. It was from a fine stock.

"I would guess that you're not married, Mr. McCoy. You wear no ring."

Spur laughed and nodded. "Right you are, so far no woman would have me. I'm a fiddlefoot at heart, a bumblebee buzzing around the pretty flowers."

"Interesting way to put it. Me Ling has our supper ready, let's go into the dining room."

The dining room was elegant, carefully furnished and decorated to rival the best rooms in New York or Washington. Thick carpet covered the floor over a pad of some kind. The dining room table was set for two but could easily seat twenty. Its polished mahogany and cherry wood gleamed through twenty coats of rubbed varnish.

An old fashioned cut glass chandelier made to hold fifty candles glowed with a dozen that had been lighted around the edges. It was a room perfectly set up by a person with an artistic eye and plenty of money to work out those ideas.

Two places were set side by side at the near end of the long table. He held her chair and then sat beside her.

"Mr. McCoy, I hope you're hungry because we're on the wild side tonight. We have bear roast, venison steaks, wild turkey and oysters for our meat course."

"I'm getting hungry already," Spur said.

The salad came first, a mixture of several vegetables with a dressing on it that was as good as the carrots and lettuce and celery and tomatoes.

"You said before that Mr. Trevarow was a friend of yours. I've heard you spend a lot of time over in his office."

"True. He's a policeman and trying to rid himself of his old fast draw reputation. It's hard for a man with a name like he had to hang up his guns."

119

Dirk Fletcher

"You are something of a fast gun yourself, aren't you, Mr. McCoy?"

"A minor talent, Mrs. Bechtel. I'd much rather be a partner in a profitable gold mine. But those making money don't want any investors, and those who want investors aren't anywhere near making any money."

Milly Bechtel laughed. For the first time Spur noticed what she wore. It was a one piece dress that was cut low for the backwoods of California, exposing the surging tops of her breasts. The dress was a pale green, reflecting the color of her eyes and contrasting with her red hair.

"You're staring at me again," she said with a laugh.

"I know, I enjoy watching a beautiful woman who knows how to dress well. An old failing of mine. New York, we were going to talk about New York. Where did you live?"

"Fifty-ninth Street and Third Avenue. There wasn't much there at the time. That was almost fifteen years ago."

"You wouldn't recognize it now, much has changed."

"My father worked on the street cars, so you see I come from humble beginnings."

"Right now you're not living humbly. This is a beautiful house, an exquisite room, better than most of the best in New York City."

"Thank you. I do what I can to be civilized, even in Bodie. I freeze every winter here. You probably won't be staying over the winter."

Spur laughed. "Does anyone stay the winter in Bodie who can get away?"

They both laughed.

A half hour later the meal was finished.

"Come, it's time you had my fifty-cent tour of the house. This isn't the only interesting room."

She showed him a huge kitchen.

"We made this by taking out two walls, adding the fireplace and the two cookstoves along that wall. We dug a well just hoping we'd have a pump right in the sink, and we do!"

The kitchen was a delight for a cook, and it smelled of fresh bread and spices and herbs.

Milly caught his hand as she led him up the open staircase to the second floor. They went past the first door then into the next one.

She swung her arm to present the view: "My bedroom," she said, looking almost shy for a moment.

Then she leaned forward and kissed his lips and pushed against him until her breasts flattened against his chest. Slowly her lips came from his but only an inch, and she held him tightly. "Spur McCoy, this is where I've been wanting to get you since the first day I saw you on the street. It took me almost an hour to find out what your name was."

She clung to him but one hand worked between them and rubbed at his crotch.

"Spur McCoy, you have a choice. You can submit to my lovemaking like a gentleman, or you can wait and let me seduce you. Either way, I hope you'll enjoy it."

This time it was Spur who bent and kissed her. He forced her head back and his tongue battered at her lips a moment until they parted and he tasted the wine from dinner.

Slowly they sank to the bed and lay side by side. Milly's eyes were closed, her hand still massaging his crotch and quickly found the start of his hardness.

"Yes, yes, yes! I can't wait to see him."

Spur's hand worked down under the bodice of her dress, lifted fabric and then circled one of her generous and now warm breasts.

"Spur, I hope I've got enough tits to satisfy you. Men always like them big."

"The ones I like best are the ones hot and pulsating in my hand," Spur said. He kissed her, guiding her onto her back, where he lay heavily on her for a moment, then sat her up.

"The dress," he said.

She stood and did a little dance for him, working it up over her hips, then to her shoulders and at last pulling it over her head, sending her hair flying. She threw the dress across the room and stripped a thin chemise over her head as well.

Her breasts were firm, with small pink areolas around ruby tipped nipples that were nearly flat. She walked up to where Spur sat and stood there, waiting.

Spur chuckled, then sucked one orb into his mouth and chewed on it like a new born babe.

"Those have to last all night, don't chew them off yet," she said, moving his head to the other morsel. She pulled away and started to undress him.

"You like me to do this?" she asked.

Spur nodded, catching a breast in each hand. "The anticipation is half the fun," McCoy said, surprised at how large and firm her breasts were. This girl was big all over.

She got his jacket and tie and shirt off, then let him remove his cowboy boots and socks.

For a moment she looked at his trousers, then she pushed him over on the bed on his back and began to kiss his erection through the cloth.

"First impressions are important," she said

smiling. "I want to see Mr. Dick here at his biggest, throbbing best."

She kissed each button off, pushed her mouth inside the open fly and blew hot air through his underwear onto his cock. Spur growled. Milly pulled down his pants, then in one quick motion jerked down his shorts.

"My god!" she crooned. "My aching pussy! Now that is what I call a worthwhile prick!"

She sent a dozen kisses up his shaft, then licked off his purple head before she sucked him into her mouth. A moment later she came off him, stood and wiggled out of the tight drawers that buttoned at the side and extended halfway down each leg.

Spur grinned when he saw the red bush at her crotch. "I'll be damned, you're a real redhead!"

"Right, more red pussy hairs than you can count."

She crawled up his body where it lay on the bed, moved higher and let her breasts swing down tantalizingly to his mouth, then moved higher until his face was directly under her red bush. Spur pulled down on her hips until his mouth found her nether lips and he licked them off until she shrilled in pleasure and climaxed, jolting sideways on the bed, her hips pounding into the covers as her whole body rattled and shook in a series of three spasms that left her panting and wailing.

She looked up in amazement. "God, McCoy! You're only the second man who ever did that for me. Most of them cut and run about then. Christ, you even look like you enjoyed sucking me off that way."

"If both of us don't enjoy it, then it's no good. Come here."

She rolled to him lifting her breasts toward his

mouth but he shook his head. He put her on her back, spread her legs and lifted her knees. Then his hand worked down through her red muff until he found the small node that he rubbed gently.

"My god, Spur! again?" Almost at once she thundered into another climax, jolting from side to side, pulling his face down on her breasts and not able to let him go.

At last Spur pushed away so he could breathe as the climax eased off. She gave a big sigh and leaned up and kissed him hard on the mouth.

"It's your turn," she said. She pulled him over her and lifted her legs to his shoulders.

"Find me," she cooed.

He did, daggering in at that unusual angle and bringing gasps of surprise and wonder from her.

"Heard it could be done but damn, what a wild feeling! Don't you ever come out of there, that's strange, wild, wonderful!"

Spur began to move, he had to move or die. Slowly he worked his shaft around and in and out and she purred, then moaned in ecstatic pleasure as the beat moved faster. Soon her hips tried to play a counterpoint as the passion grew.

"Oh, my god! Oh, my god! Oh, my god!" she squealed. Spur hurried then, blasting into her hard and fast as he felt his own peak nearing. She shouted and he bellowed in release as they both climaxed at the same time, a shuddering pounding, thrashing melee of arms and legs on the bed.

When they both came down from the peaks, they lay half off the bed and edged back on it, then collapsed in wonder and joy and peace.

"Darling Spur McCoy, there is nothing in the whole world that is as good as what just happened. Nothing in life. This is the ultimate experience of the humanoid. There's nowhere else to go, no worlds to conquer, no rivers to cross. Damn, but I tend to get philosophical when making love has been extremely wonderful. But it doesn't happen often, not this good. We'd make one hell of a team, in and out of bed."

"I don't know anything about gold mines."

"Neither do I. I hire men who know, who can do the job and make money. I manage money."

"I don't have any of that at all."

"No, no, silly man. The trick is to use other people's money. I didn't have a dime when Warren married me. Now I'm worth several hundred thousand. Making more all the time. How's that for a dowry?"

"I could always rob a gold shipment. That would give me a nice little nest egg."

"Too risky. They always get caught."

"This bunch this week hasn't. I hear they got away free and clear. Nobody even has a clue who they might be."

"We'll wait and see. It's still too risky. I married my money."

"You looking for a new husband?"

"No, only a stud who can fuck me as good as you did tonight. Want the job?"

"Got a job, back east—but it's an interesting proposition. Are you always this good in bed?"

"Always, sometimes better, but not often. You?"

"It's always good for me."

Milly rang a small bell on a bedside table. The bedroom door opened and Spur looked for something to cover himself with but Milly laughed.

"Spur, you're dressed properly for the occasion. Look."

Me Ling opened the door fully and smiled. She

was as naked as they were. She brought in a whiskey bottle and a pitcher of water and carefully poured two fingers of whiskey in each of three glasses, then filled them halfway with water.

She was so slender and curveless she could be mistaken for a boy. Mature but tiny, almost flat breasts gave the only hint of her womanhood. A soft dark triangle of hair nestled in her crotch.

"Me Ling has come to play," Milly said. "Often the two of us play together, but it's more fun to share a man between us. Would you like to be between us, McCoy?"

Already Me Ling was at his crotch urging him back to the proper condition. It took her only a minute. Me Ling squealed in delight as he came up strong and stiff. She caught his hand and put it over her small breast.

"Me Ling speaks almost no English, and never when we play. Now the only way you can communicate is by touch."

Spur stroked her legs, then pushed his hand between them and one lifted into the air opening her heartland to him.

Before Spur realized what she was doing, she had bent and caught his erection and sucked all of it into her mouth. She began bobbing her head up and down. Quickly he pulled her away before he lost his control.

Spur turned and watched Milly who sat beside him. "Just what kind of games do you want to play now?"

Milly smiled. "Any kind of games that three can play. But first it's Me Ling's turn with you, then we do something different and creative. You be thinking up the ways."

It was nearly four A.M. when Spur came away

from the finely built house and walked toward his hotel. There was no one on the street. He was exhausted, but remembering the remarkable things the small Chinese girl could do.

Behind him in her bedroom, Milly Bechtel watched Spur until she was sure he was going to the hotel. She frowned into the mirror at her naked form, then thought about Spur McCoy.

She took three deep breaths reasoning it through. It was nothing he had said, it was a feeling she had. And in the past her feelings had almost always been right. She went to a door that led into an adjoining room and roused a man who slept in a large bed.

"Wake up, Deadman," she said. "Come on sleepyhead, time to get up. You have a job to do."

"Huh? What time is it?"

"Morning, as far as you're concerned," Milly said. She sat on the edge of the bed.

"Still dark out."

"Good, then it should be easier for you. I have another job for you. You better be good, Billy Deadman, because I know this other guy is damn fast. Before tomorrow night I want you to kill Spur McCoy. He didn't accuse me of anything, but something doesn't feel right. He knows too much. I think he's more than he admits, maybe even some kind of a lawman. That should give you extra incentive, Deadman.

"Now get that pretty naked body of yours out of bed, get your pants on and kill Spur McCoy before the sun comes up—if you can."

8

Billy Deadman reached for the naked woman, but she slipped away.

"Not now," Milly Bechtel said with a hint of regret. "Just as soon as you kill Spur McCoy we'll do anything you want, any way you want!"

Billy nodded and dressed slowly and with care as he always did. He made sure of everything as he went, nothing was ever left to chance. That was how he had stayed alive for so long.

Deadman asked Milly where the hardware store was, left by her back door and five minutes later pried off the simple lock on the back of the store and stepped inside. He used matches to find what he wanted in the back: a steel box that contained a carton of dynamite sticks.

He'd used them before, lots of times. He took three sticks, tied them together with wire, then found the detonator caps outside the steel container and took one from the sack. He pushed it into one stick of the powder and inserted a foot long fuse in the outer hollow half of the detonator. Then he left the hardware, not bothering to cover up anything and leaving the back door unlocked.

That afternoon he had made certain what room in the U.S. Hotel Spur McCoy had rented. It always paid to think ahead. He had the second one over from the center on the second floor. He figured Milly might want Spur taken out, and Billy was always ready to do a job when the money was right. Some in town said McCoy was fast with a six-gun. No sense taking a deadly chance when it wasn't required.

Deadman watched Main Street for five minutes. He saw no deputies walking and checking doors. Nothing moved. He was in a doorway a building down from the U.S. Hotel.

Now he walked naturally from the store and in front of the hotel. When he was directly below the window he wanted, he paused at the side of the building and lit a cigar. At the same time he lit the dynamite fuse and let it burn while he counted to twenty. He had cut a foot long length of fuse, so it should burn for a minute. Deadman knew he dared not let the fuse burn too long.

Now!

He took three steps into the street until he could see the window, threw the bomb with enough force to break the glass. The dynamite smashed the window and landed inside. Deadman walked down to the corner and then ran along the side of the hotel in the darkness. He was half a block away when the blast went off.

Deadman walked through the darkness of the alley until he came to the Bechtel house and went in the back door. Milly sat at the big kitchen table. She wore a warm robe. She had started a fire and boiled two cups of coffee. She poured him one.

He gulped down some of the hot brew, then threw the cup across the room and grabbed her, ripping open the robe to be sure she was naked underneath. He pushed her shoulders down forcing her to the kitchen floor.

"Right here?" she asked.

"Damn right, right here!" he barked. "Killing people makes me feel just sexy as all damnation!"

When Spur McCoy stumbled into his room shortly after four A.M. he thought something seemed different. He wasn't sure enough to do anything about it. The truth was he had consumed far too much of Milly Bechtel's sweet mash whiskey and the added drain of having sex several times with two not only willing but insatiable ladies, left him not quite sober and extremely tired.

He fell into bed, reached for his .45 where it usually hung when he dressed up for a night with a lady, but didn't find it. Before he could get up to look, he slept.

An explosion a few minutes later roused him but he didn't fully awaken. He heard a lot of yelling and shouts, but no one banged on his door so he went back to sleep.

With morning came his pounding head and he pulled the cover over his head and slept until noon. Then he got up and looked around.

He was in the wrong room. He must have been drunker than he figured. Spur gathered up his clothes, opened the door and looked down the hall. No one was there. He went back to the stairway, found room 204 and started to go in.

There was no door. It lay shattered against the opposite hall wall. The inside of the room was blackened and in tatters and showered with plaster from the ceiling. The window had been broken out. He smelled the familiar odor of cordite and blasting powder. Someone had bombed his room last night after he got to sleep in the wrong spot.

Spur found his gun hanging undamaged on the bedpost. From what he could tell the bomb had come in the window and rolled toward the bed. The mattress had absorbed some of the blast, but still the room was a disaster.

He put on a pair of more serviceable pants, stuffed a shirt inside, then buckled on his gun and gathered up what was left of his carpetbag and his clothes. He took all his belongings back to room 6 where he had spent the night. Then he marched downstairs and complained about the blast in his room.

The man behind the counter had gone white for a moment when he saw Spur, then caught his breath. "Mr. McCoy, you're alive!"

"No thanks to that bomb last night. You know who threw it in the window?"

"No sir. But how . . . how did you stay alive in there?"

"That's my little secret. I'm now in room 6, but don't record it and don't tell a soul, not even the manager, or I'll strip your tongue out and beat you to death with it. Not a word!"

Spur had two cups of coffee and a bowl of oatmeal for his breakfast and lunch, then about one o'clock headed for the jail.

Just outside the hotel he almost bumped into Billy Deadman who stared at him in surprise, then anger.

Deadman walked past him, then spun around.

"Yeah, you're Spur McCoy!" Deadman barked.

Spur stopped and turned slowly. "I don't think we've met," Spur said carefully, knowing the man and his reputation.

"No, we've never met, but only because you were to yellow to call me out. I've seen you draw. You're about fast enough to outdraw my old maid aunt. She's eighty-four and in a wheel chair."

"My friends were right about you, Deadman. You're not only vulgar and stupid, you're ugly, too."

Deadman grinned. "Now that's not a nice thing to say, little man. Would you care to back up those words with that hogleg of yours?"

"Why should you die so early in the day, Deadman? Are you the jackass who threw that bomb in my window last night? You're the only one in Bodie shit-dumb enough to do it."

"I'm calling you out, McCoy!" Deadman screamed. "Nobody talks to me that way and lives! You're a dead man, you don't know it yet! Right now, right here!"

Spur let his right hand fall to his side. He shifted his feet apart a little more and stared at Deadman.

"It was you with the bomb, wasn't it? Who paid you to try to kill me, you yellow bellied river rat?"

"I did it as a public service!" Deadman bellowed.

They stood thirty feet apart now, facing each other. Deadman had moved to the middle of the street and Spur angled the same way. People behind each man scattered. Doors down Main Street slammed shut. One man dropped shutters over his big plate glass window.

"Anytime you're ready to die, asshole!" Deadman thundered.

A moment later a shotgun roared, then a voice

jolted into the silence that followed it.

"Hold it! Both of you. This is Captain Trevarow. I've just banned gunplay in the city limits. No stand downs, no gunfights, no fast draws. Both of you look at the sidewalk. There's a shotgun on each one of us. Either man goes for his gun, one of my deputies will blow your legs right out from under you with a load of birdshot. Won't kill you, but you'll walk with lead in your ass for the rest of your life.

"Now, easy like, both of you take your weapons out with a thumb and finger and drop them on the ground. Do it now, dammit!"

Spur looked at Trevarow and saw that he held a shotgun, too.

Deadman stared at Spur. "This your set up, McCoy?"

"Don't know anything about it, Deadman."

Slowly the two gunmen reached for their weapons, unseated them with finger and thumb and as if on signal, dropped them in the dust.

There was no question what would happen next. Both roared like bull bears and charged forward. Spur sidestepped the slightly bigger man's charge and slammed a fist into the back of his neck.

Deadman roared in pain and anger and spun, only to find Spur on top of him with two short hard jabs with his right fist and a roundhouse left that caught Deadman on the point of his chin. The big man staggered back a moment, shook his head and charged forward.

Spur landed two hard jabs on Deadman's nose, breaking it and bringing a gush of blood, but the heavier man's progress seemed slowed not at all as he thundered into Spur, grabbed him around the back with his hands and then tripped. They fell and rolled in the dust and directly over some horse droppings.

The fall broke Deadman's grip and Spur jumped up. There was no reason for the men to inform each other that there were no holds barred, anything went: eye gouging, ball busting, ear tearing.

Spur changed his tactics. As soon as Deadman levered to his feet, Spur charged and jumped, slamming both feet into Deadman's unprotected chest. Deadman spilled backwards, caught off balance and sprawled in the dirt. Spur dropped to his hands and knees and was up in an instant.

Deadman shook his head to clear it. The kick to his chest had rattled him more than hurt him. He had never seen anyone fight that way before. Spur had boxed on the team at Harvard, and two years ago had an old Chinese in San Francisco teach him the basic arts of self defense using feet and hands as weapons. He had learned only two or three kicks and a few hand movements, but they had proved effective.

Deadman got up on his hands and knees, then pushed to his feet and circled Spur. He rushed forward and threw a handful of dust into Spur's eyes. He had picked it up when he was down. Spur saw it coming, closed his eyes, but still some of it got into his eyes. Deadman charged, caught Spur in a bear hug again. Spur butted him in the face with his head, then when Deadman increased the pressure of the squeeze, Spur lifted both his hands and clapped his palms together on both of Deadman's ears at the same time.

The tremendous increase in pressure slamming into the delicate bones in Deadman's head broke his hold and he screamed in agony of the pain.

Spur moved in at once, kicked him in the stomach,

then slammed rights and lefts into Deadman's jaw until he wavered. Spur doubled up both hands into one fist and used it like a hammer to pound a mighty blow down on the back of Deadman's exposed neck.

He went down and out.

A cheer went up from the two hundred people who had crowded around to watch a real grudge fight. There hadn't been one in the street in daylight for nearly a month.

Spur found his brown, low crowned hat, the one with the Mexican silver pesos around the headband, and walked carefully over to the store fronts and sat in a chair. A deputy brought him his six-gun.

"Captain Trevarow says you better come down to the jail until Deadman cools off," the deputy said. "Deadman won't take this without trying to kill you for sure."

"It would have been over by now if he hadn't butted in. You tell him . . ." Spur stopped. "Yeah, he might be right. I want some clean clothes, and to wash my face. Tell Trevarow I'll be down there directly."

Spur went back to the hotel, feeling every blow and bruise he had just received. He went up to his new room, washed up and changed his shirt, then made sure his gunbelt was full of rounds and pushed a box of fifty more in his pocket.

The deputy was right about one thing, Deadman wouldn't take a beating and walk away from it. He'd want satisfaction on the end of a blazing six-gun. It was time Spur gave him the chance.

Spur checked his weapon. He cleaned it, making sure the cylinder was well oiled and functioning perfectly. The action was smooth and fast. Then he holstered the weapon, checked the curl of his brown hat and went out the door.

His next stop was at the Kirkwood Stable where he rented a good horse and saddle. He would use it this afternoon and tonight as well on the gold run. First he had to deal with Deadman.

He rode back down Main and found Deadman walking along, watching every face he met.

"Over here, Deadman," Spur called.

Deadman looked up.

"Get yourself a horse. I'll meet you just outside of town to the south whenever you get up nerve enough to ride out."

Deadman swore and started to draw, but Spur was out of any kind of range. He glowered, then pushed his weapon back in leather.

"Yeah, half an hour, McCoy. You figure out what you want on your grave marker!"

Deadman asked a man on the street something, then rushed down the street toward the livery.

Spur rode out of town slowly. It would take Deadman a half hour to get a horse and ride out. He stopped at a well at the bottle works for a drink of cold water, then continued out to the rise that overlooked the town. Spur got off his mount, a sturdy bay, and quieted her, then walked around kicking rocks.

Yes, he was stupid to give Deadman a chance at him, but he'd learned that with a man like Deadman it was better to get it over with. If he didn't make it a fair fight, Deadman would bushwhack him the first chance when he stepped out of the hotel, or out of a saloon, and nobody would know who killed him.

This way it could be over quickly, one way or another. He knew Deadman was fast. Maybe it wouldn't come to that. Once he got out here away from the crowd, Deadman might act differently. But would it be more rational, or wild and crazy?

Spur saw Deadman coming, cantering along at a good pace as if he were eager to get started on the killing.

Spur mounted up, checked his six-gun in his holster and waited.

Deadman stopped fifty yards away and stared at McCoy. "You really ready to die, Spur McCoy?"

"About as ready as you are. You still want to go through with this? You can ride for Bridgeport and nothing will be said."

Deadman laughed. "Not a chance."

He swung up a rifle from his boot and pulled it to his shoulder. Spur dove off his horse to the right, keeping the animal between him and the rifle. That son-of-a-bitch!

The rifle snarled once, then quickly again, and Spur realized that Deadman had a repeating rifle. Spur hit the rocks and dirt on both hands and knees, then his shoulder as he rolled. He clawed at his six-gun to make sure it stayed in place.

Damn! He had trusted this bastard and he probably would die for that trust!

He heard the first round thud into the bay. She let out a bellow, then the second round hit her as she was falling and she screamed as she hit the ground and kicked the air in a death struggle.

Spur rolled away from the horse and searched for some cover. There was almost none. A rain run off gully barely two feet deep cut through the side of the hill. Spur rolled into that and lifted his six-gun over the lip of dirt. He could see Deadman walking his horse slowly forward.

He would come as close as he could and stay out of range of the six-gun. Spur had made shots with a pistol at fifty yards, but the elevation needed made it a guessing game. Still, if that was all Deadman left him.

Spur knew he would not lay there and let Deadman come up and drill him with rifle rounds. As soon as Spur had an open shot at Deadman past the dead horse, he tried. He lifted the muzzle of the Colt and sighted in. There was almost no wind today.

Spur fired. He saw Deadman jolt and swing the horse back a few yards. The singing .45 slug had come close enough to worry Deadman. That was something.

"I got all afternoon, McCoy. I can come in and finish you off anytime I want to."

Spur decided on the silent approach. He crawled down hill where the little ditch became deeper. Fifty yards down it grew into a ravine six feet deep. Spur kept low so Deadman could not see him and crawled along the ditch.

"Where the hell are you, McCoy, you coward. You afraid to face me?"

Spur kept moving. Every foot of distance he got down the little gully gave him more cover, more options, more operating room. He kept his six-gun in his hand for instant action if Deadman rode up fast.

Every minute, every second now gave him better odds at living.

Spur heard Deadman's horse galloping along the small ravine but not quite close enough to spot him.

McCoy came to a place where a small sage bush grew above the side of the gully. Spur pushed up two feet and peered over the dirt at where he thought the rider might be.

The gunman sat on his horse, staring in the other direction. He still held the rifle with the butt on his thigh and the barrel in the air. It was also ready for instant action—instant death.

Spur crawled again.

His strategic position was bad. Sooner or later Deadman would figure out that he was in the gully and he would simply ride down it until he saw Spur and gun him down with the rifle staying well out of pistol range. Spur had to get him close enough so he could kill Deadman's horse if not him. The horse would be an easier target at thirty to forty yards.

As he worked down the grade, Spur could now lift up to his hands and knees. He looked ahead toward the bottling works and the first few houses on this side of town. They were still a quarter of a mile away. He would never make it before he was ridden down.

His mind reeled back to years before and he thought of the time he was in Arizona tangling with the Chiricahua Apache. Yes, the in-plain-sight trick!

Now he looked at the bottom of the small ravine. It was over three feet from the top. At this point it flattened out a little and there was a deposit of silt and sand and probably some gold dust in the sand. How deep was it?

Quickly he began digging with his hands. He lay the pistol to one side within easy reach and dug. Five minutes later he had a section eight inches deep, a foot wide and six feet long. He needed another ten minutes. Furiously he dug with his hands in the soft sand. Then he sat down in the hole he had dug and stretched out his legs in the ditch in the sand. Quickly he covered his feet and legs with the sand he had dug out until it was nearly flat.

Now he covered his hips and as he stretched out on his back in the ditch like crater, he kept covering himself with sand until only one arm was free. He used a thin handkerchief over his face and sprinkled it with the sand lightly to cover it, yet allow him to see through.

His left arm was under the sand and his shoulders and head. His right arm was hardest. He had to keep it ready for a quick shot, yet still out of sight. At last he burrowed it into the warm sand with another handkerchief over the weapon itself filtered by a skiff of sand.

He relaxed. The trap was in place. Either Deadman would find him, not be fooled and kill him quickly, or he had a chance to surprise the gunman.

Spur held his breath as he heard a galloping horse. The beast went by fast on the left side of the gully. Spur saw Deadman looking at the ravine, but staring mostly downstream. Twenty feet down the bend in the small runoff the arroyo straightened and Deadman could see it for the quarter of a mile where it emptied into what sometimes was Bodie Creek. He saw that Spur had not moved down that way.

The rider stopped and stared back along the ditch. Slowly Deadman turned and walked his mount back toward where McCoy lay. He was not even looking at the bottom of the ditch. Evidently Deadman had decided that McCoy was not there. He probably was trying to figure out where the man had disappeared to.

Spur held his body rigid for a moment, then relaxed.

The horseman came closer. Fifty feet. Too far.

Spur watched through the haze of the sand on the handkerchief. Thirty feet. Not yet.

McCoy breathed softly, then held his breath and tightened his grip on the .44. He prayed that the sand had not got into the cylinder works on the Colt. Twenty feet.

When the big horse and rider were directly beside Spur, not six feet away, Spur lifted up from the sand in one heave, screamed an Apache war cry and fired four times at the man and the horse towering ten feet over him.

Spur saved two rounds. He saw the first hit the man in the thigh. It was a terrible angle for a killing shot. From his low position he couldn't even see Deadman's head or torso. The second round missed high, the third hit the horse in the side of the head, and the forth hit the animal's head as well.

As soon as he fired the shots, Spur surged up from the ground in one fluid motion, charged down the ravine twenty feet and slid to a stop as he dropped down under cover again.

He lifted up and peered over the edge of the rocky soil toward the rider. He saw the horse down and kicking in a death struggle. Spur never liked killing a horse, but better the horse than Spur McCoy. It simply had to be done. He watched for any human movement.

A body rolled away from the downed horse. Spur snapped a shot but missed. He reloaded his Colt, putting six rounds into the chambers, and letting the hammer down gently.

Where was Deadman?

Did Deadman still have the repeating rifle?

Deadman stood and looked at Spur. He was out of pistol range. He shook his fist.

"You bastard! You killed my horse, you jammed my rifle. But I'll hunt you down and kill you with my bare hands if I have to."

He turned and jogged to the west, away from town toward some higher hills and rugged canyon.

Spur followed him at a safe range. What was Deadman trying to do? Twice Spur sprinted over a flat place, trying to get within pistol range, but each time Deadman saw him coming and ran faster to keep out of range.

At last Spur saw the plan. Deadman headed for a rocky, boulder strewn gully a half mile ahead. There were a few spindly shrubs but no real trees. What did he hope to gain there?

As they came closer, Spur understood.

Cover.

Deadman would be first into the boulder strewn gully. He would have the advantage of selection and he also could find cover and command the entrance to the canyon. He could get in a position where Spur would have to expose himself to a killing shot to advance any farther.

Twenty minutes later, Deadman vanished into the boulders. Spur sprinted at right angles to the route Deadman had taken so he could enter the boulders fifty yards away from where Deadman wanted him to. If he moved quickly enough Deadman would not have time to duplicate his lateral movement.

As he ran he pumped his arms and sucked in every bit of the rarified atmosphere that he could. He was never a gifted runner at sea level. At 8,500 or 9,000 feet, the air is much thinner and has much less oxygen than the usual 21 percent. Spur soon felt the lack of oxygen to his muscles.

He panted and gasped as he raced behind the first large boulder forty yards from where Deadman had entered. For the moment he was safe and he now had equal tactical advantage.

In the game of hide and seek where the loser dies, a man is extremely careful in his movements. Spur knew the odds. He had never been in quite this situation before. He climbed to the top of the boulder and looked over. Thirty yards ahead he spotted Deadman beginning to climb up the big rock he hid behind.

Spur dropped down before Deadman saw him and moved to the side of his protection, then darted forward almost ten yards to another boulder before Deadman got into position to see him.

The advantage! He had it now. He knew where Deadman was, and the gunman had no idea where Spur was. He peered around the side of the boulder without his hat on and saw Deadman flat on top of his rock. The range was still too great.

He watched again and as soon as Deadman slid back out of sight, Spur dashed ahead to the next cover he had selected which was no more than ten yards from Deadman. When he got there he would wait and let Deadman walk into his gunsights.

Spur settled down in his new position, his weapon up and ready. Five minutes went by and Spur began to wonder if he had figured Deadman right. Then he heard a rock kicked ahead. There were two smaller boulders between the large ones. Both were the kind a man would have to sprawl out behind to get good cover.

Another minute passed, then Deadman stepped out from behind the big rock, his six-gun ahead of him, eyes alert. At first he missed seeing Spur where he lay at the base of the big rock behind a blush of green grass. When he found him his .44 came down and then he laughed.

Spur had heard the slight rattling at the same time. Without moving his head he looked in front of him and a foot to the right and saw a coiled rattle-snake, its tail rattling gently. It was merely curious. Twin black eyes stared at him and the forked tongue darted out to sense if this creature was dangerous.

Spur couldn't move. If he did the reptile would strike him. It was barely eighteen inches away from his face, half that from his gunhand.

"Well now, looks like Mother Nature did me a little favor," Deadman brayed. "You would have gunned me down without warning, if our little friend there hadn't got the drop on you. McCoy, sometimes luck runs all bad. That Indian trick was great, but you should have killed me instead of just hitting my leg."

He laughed again. "Yeah, no sense wasting a three cent round on you McCoy. We'll see how long you can wait out that rattler without moving. I'll give you about three minutes, then you'll try something. Course the second you try to move, snake eyes there will nail you. I'll just sit down here and wait and watch."

Deadman sat down without taking his gaze off Spur and the snake. The man was right. Spur knew he could stay still for ten minutes if he had to. But it wouldn't matter. Even if he outbluffed the snake, Deadman would gun him the second the snake left.

Alternate attack plan. New strategy. What had he done in the Civil War? Nothing came to mind.

"Ease off there, McCoy. You're a dead man either way, just watch and wait and enjoy your last few minutes on this blessed green earth."

Spur watched him. He hated the smug, all knowing look that the gunman wore. A movement to the right of Deadman caught Spur's attention. He checked it and looked away. The triangular head of a large rattler had edged within an inch of Deadman's hip. When Spur checked back the large rattler had coiled so close he was almost touching the man's left hip. The beady eyes studied this new element in its living space.

"I'd say another two minutes, maybe, McCoy. Want to confess anything, or have me send your belongings to a next of kin?" Deadman laughed. "Hell, I wouldn't do that anyway. Certainly not any cash you might have hidden on you."

"You're the one who should worry, Deadman. There's the biggest rattler I've ever seen coiled an inch away from your hip. I don't think the big guy trusts you."

"Good try, Spur. I figured you could do better than that. You mind if I light up a good cigar and don't give you one? I enjoy a good cigar after I do a killing." His left hand slid down toward his pocket.

In a movement so fast Spur could barely follow it, the rattler's head struck the hated human arm three times. The last time it couldn't get its fangs out. As soon as he realized he had been bitten, Deadman tried to leap to his feet. He stumbled, his .45 discharged into the rock and then he lost the weapon.

The moment the gunshot sounded, Spur's rattler turned to check the danger from behind. Spur saw the change in angle of the deadly head near him and he moved his six-gun and fired, blowing the rattler's head off its body.

Deadman screamed the second the first strike poured the rattlesnake venom into his wrist. He struggled to his feet and shook his arm to dislodge the snake, then kicked at it as it slithered off into a rocky hole between two boulders. The creature was more than six feet long and as big around as a grown man's arm.

Spur came to his feet, checked for more rattlers then looked at Deadman.

Deadman leaned against the rock.

"I'd say you were in deep-shit trouble, Mister Deadman. How many strikes, three or four?"

Deadman didn't hear the words. He dug for his knife, but instead of attacking Spur, he made a slit on his wrist over one of the bites.

"Suck the poison out!" Deadman shouted. "Yeah, I heard that you cut the fang mark and suck out the blood and spit it out." He stared at the slice he had made on his wrist. "Damn that hurts!" He bent and sucked at the cut, then spit and sucked again.

Spur found Deadman's gun and pushed it under his gun belt.

"I heard that sucking idea works once or twice out of about fifty bites," Spur said. "Not that I want to discourage you."

"Shut up!" Deadman screamed. He looked at his wrist, then back toward Bodie. "I'll hurry and get to Doc Rogers. Let him do the cutting. He's got that little suction cup thing."

"Walking back to Bodie would be the worst thing you could do," Spur said. "That will speed up your heart, and your circulation, and move the poison deeper through your system where it will kill you."

"Then I'll run, get there faster!"

Deadman came past Spur, headed for the open land and soon was jogging along toward Bodie. In their pistolero standoff they had worked almost two miles from the town. Spur figured Deadman would get about halfway. Spur trailed along behind him, watching and waiting.

Deadman only made it a half mile, then got so dizzy he had to sit on the ground for a while. When his vision cleared he ran again, but a hundred yards later he screamed and fell into the dirt.

"I can't see!" Deadman bellowed.

"It'll clear up in a minute. How's your arm?"

"Hurts like hell." He looked at it. Already it had swollen up over the bites. It had turned red. "Hot, it's also hot and hurts like it's on fire!"

"I told you not to run, Deadman. But you know everything."

"Yeah, everything. How come you didn't die in that bomb blast?"

"I was in another room last night."

"Just my luck."

"Like you told me, Deadman, sometimes you get a run of luck but it's all bad. Seems to be your problem."

"Yeah. Hey, will you carry me into town?"

"Never make it, you ran too far. Lift your left arm."

Deadman tried and couldn't. Tears streamed down his face. He screamed out all of his frustrations and anger.

"I've gunned down some of the best in my time, and now I get beat by a damn rattlesnake?"

"Looks like it."

Deadman tried to stand. He at last got to his feet and stumbled toward town a half dozen steps, then plunged into the dirt face first.

He rolled over sobbing. "Christ, oh Christ! The pain is like nothing I've ever felt. I can't take it. Shoot me, McCoy. End it for me!"

"I'm not an executioner, Deadman. Although I'm sure you deserve to be killed."

"McCoy, how long will it take. I can't even move my legs now."

"Two hours, maybe three."

"You stay here?"

"Nothing else to do until midnight. You know anything about the stage gold robbery?"

"Hell, no. Not my style."

They sat there in the dirt for a few minutes.

Deadman screamed. "McCoy, you've got to kill me. At least give me my gun and one round."

Spur stood, let out a deep breath. It was what he would want in the same situation. The poison was too far into the man's system. Not one bite, but three, maybe four. Nothing could save him now, not even Doc Rogers.

Spur took Deadman's pistol from his belt, opened the cylinder and emptied out all but one round. He moved the cylinder so the loaded round would be the next to fire.

"Put your hand over your shoulder and I'll give you the weapon. Best way to make sure is to eat the muzzle. Push it to the top of your mouth. Can't miss that way."

Spur watched him a minute. "You sure you want it this way?"

"Yes, dammit!" Deadman said. His speech was slurred now.

"You try to gun me with that one round and I'll shoot you where it hurts, but I won't kill you. Understand?"

"Yes."

Spur extended the muzzle of the weapon over Deadman's shoulder from behind him. It took Deadman three tries to grab the barrel. When he had it, Spur walked away from the dying man.

Deadman made no attempt to shoot Spur. With great difficulty he turned the weapon around, holding it in his right hand. He made two tries before he got the muzzle in his mouth.

Then almost at once a muffled shot slammed through the rocks and hills above Bodie, California.

Deadman's head jolted back and upward as the

large lead slug smashed through the roof of his mouth and into his brain. It shattered ten vital brain complex centers, then bored out through his skull taking a four-square inch chunk with it.

9

It took the rest of the afternoon for Captain
Trevarow and Spur to get the body to Hooperman
and return the saddles and tack to the livery. Spur
paid $25 for his dead horse and told Kirkwood at the
livery to bill the county for the other horse.

Back in the office, Spur and Trevarow worked out
which men would be assigned to ride with Spur on
the gold run.

"You want five deputies so you can trail along in
back of the stage?"

"Right, John. If we knew where the killers would
hit the stage we could go there and wait, but we
don't. They could take it any of a dozen places, the
driver told me."

"You want the men saddled and ready at 9:30 in
back of the Kirkwood livery, right?"

"Yes, and each man should carry a Spencer
repeating rifle and fifty rounds."

"That we can do. Just don't get none of my boys

shot up."

"Do my best. Right now I'm going to catch some sleep. We'll be up all night, I'd guess."

That night a little before ten P.M. Spur met the gold stage after it had moved well away from the gold pickup point at Bechtel Mine #3. The stage driver sat on the top seat and waved at Spur in the darkness.

"Got to talk to all of you a few minutes," Spur said. The driver stopped the rig and the guards looked out.

"Tonight we're going to be robbed, I'd bet my horse on it. I've talked to Mr. Johnson at Wells Fargo. They're paying you to defend this shipment. But tonight, we want to get held up and cleaned out."

He heard the guards whispering.

"We think we know who robbed the last stage and killed those eight men. But to prove it we have to let them rob you again. The secret this time is don't put up too hard a fight. Try to miss the attackers if you shoot. Make certain you don't kill anybody. Everyone have that straight?"

"Tonight we get robbed."

"How we know they won't take the stage over, then shoot all of us like last time?" a guard asked from inside.

"Good question. That's why I and five deputy sheriffs will be trailing along behind you. We'll be out of sight but we'll be there. As soon as we hear shooting we'll close in fast. If they start to shoot anybody, we'll blast them and take our chances on proving who they are. I don't think they'll hurt any of you. They want the gold, not more trouble about dead guards."

Spur waited and watched them. When nobody complained he moved on.

"Any man who wants to quit this trip can do so right now, no questions asked, no problems with hiring on again. Anybody want out?"

He waited and no one spoke.

"All right, let's get moving. Keep everything as usual, natural. The driver can stay inside or outside, your option. I'd suggest you stay inside, then to stop the rig all they have to do is shoot one of the lead horses. Let's roll!"

Spur met the sheriff's deputies in back of the livery and told them exactly what they were going to do. All seemed a bit grim faced as they rode out. They trailed the stage keeping it in sight for the first five miles as they headed out of town north toward Aurora on the way to Carson City, Nevada.

Another mile and Spur slowed his men until they couldn't see the stage in the darkness. The stage rolled at its usual pace along the rough road, wound around the ridge and down the other side.

There weren't any trees here to cover the robbers. Spur had been over the route, and he breathed a little faster when the stage passed the first danger point, a steep upgrade.

Nothing happened. He moved his troops up a little closer now as the stage rolled down hill, made a sharp turn at the bottom to go across a dry stream bed and then a run through a hill speckled with eight and ten foot high boulders. This was danger point number two.

Spur heard the first shot, a rifle, that rang loudly in the quiet night air. The sound of the screaming animal came almost on top of it, and the familiar sound of the rattling stage ahead of him slowed and then stopped suddenly.

A dozen more shots blasted into the scene and Spur and his men walked their mounts forward so the robbers couldn't hear them coming.

They were at the very edge of visibility when Spur stopped them. He edged his mount ahead along the side of the road. Now he could see the robbers. Six mounted men had the stage surrounded. He wasn't sure if anyone inside had fired a shot.

Some of the robbers laughed. Few words were spoken. Voices could be remembered. He saw the strong box tossed off the stage. It smashed on the road but didn't open. Three pistol shots later the robbers cheered and Spur saw them distributing the gold bars into the saddlebags.

He tensed. Now would be the time to murder the guards if they wanted to. Instead the riders all mounted up, fired pistols in the air and turned back toward Bodie.

Spur dug his heels into his horse and rushed back toward his deputies. He motioned for them to move into the boulder area well off both sides of the trail.

"Hide! They're coming this way." Spur said quietly.

The last man had just ridden behind a big boulder when the robbers came galloping down the trail. They were singing and shouting, hoorahing as they swept past, evidently delighted by the easy robbery and hoping they would get paid extra.

When the riders went past, Spur and a deputy called Jones moved after them. McCoy had instructed the other lawmen to come along slowly behind. Six sets of hoofbeats behind the robbers could be heard.

Spur and Jones rode hard for a moment to catch

up, then when they could hear the riders ahead, they slowed. After a quarter of a mile gallop, the raiders eased off and let their mounts walk. Spur and Jones followed their example, staying far enough back in the darkness in the open land so they couldn't be seen, but close enough so they wouldn't lose touch with the six outlaws.

At four miles per hour, the two groups worked back toward Bodie. Spur watched the stars and figured by the position of the Big Dipper on its way around the North Star, that it must be nearly twelve midnight. They should be back in Bodie before one if they kept going at this rate.

Suddenly Spur held up his hand and he and Jones stopped. The men ahead were making no noise. He listened. A saddle creaked. Then the sounds came again. Men laughing, saddles groaning as men moved in or out of them.

"Pass that damn bottle over here!" a voice shouted. Then everyone laughed.

"Best two hundred dollars I ever made," another voice said. The voices kept sounding ahead, evidently as a bottle passed from one hand to another.

About five minutes later a stronger voice sounded.

"All right, that's enough. Let's ride back to town so I can pay you off. Mount up."

They all moved again. Spur walked his mount forward slowly, then faster until he had them in the fuzzy, hazy half light from the quarter sliver of a moon.

He and Jones followed them for another hour, then they stopped.

The leader's voice came clearly. "Listen to me!

Bodie's about half a mile ahead. I'd just as soon
none of you stayed in Bodie tonight. Head for
Bridgeport. They've got some new girls there, I
hear."

Some shouts went up.

"Come by me one at a time and I'll pay you, but
first I have to get all of the gold bars in my saddle
bags. Come up now and deliver."

All was quiet for a while. Then the stronger voice
came again.

"Now, I've got it all. Come by for your pay."

As each man got his money he whooped a yell and
rode off.

Spur counted five men leave, then he and Jones
moved forward slowly. Ahead in the dimness, Spur
saw a lone man and a horse. The horse had its
saddlebags stuffed full and a gunny sack evidently
holding gold bars tied to the saddle. The man
walked beside the horse down the hill toward Bodie.

McCoy wasn't surprised to see the robber leading
his horse toward the area well up on the slope where
the Bechtel mine showed in the moonlight.

Captain Trevarow had promised to have three or
four men watching the back approaches to the
Bechtel Mine #3, just in case. The plan was to let the
robber go inside the mine buildings, then they would
have the evidence they needed. Spur and Jones
moved cautiously following the robber with all the
gold.

When they came to the first buildings, Spur and
Jones left their mounts and moved in shadows and
along the sides of buildings as the man walking the
horse headed for the retort room.

He paused outside, looked around, then put the
bars of gold in the gunny sack from the saddle bags,

Eli found some heavy twine and tied all three men's wrists and ankles. He had put a bandage of sorts around his shoulder to stop the bleeding.

Mrs. Bechtel picked up Spur's weapon and the Captain's as well. She pointed to a small wheel-barrow. "Eli, put the gold in there and let's go for a walk."

Spur watched them go outside. There was still a lantern burning in the retort room. He tested the knots. They were tight.

"Jones, how you doing?" Spur asked.

"Hurts like hell. Missed my heart at least."

"Hang on. John, can you roll over here so I can untie your hands?"

"Worth a try."

It took them nearly ten minutes to maneuver around and for Spur to untie the Sheriff's Captain's hands. Then he freed the other two. Spur edged open the outside door and watched, but saw no movement. "Jones, you better go get that shot looked at. Can you walk?"

Jones nodded.

Spur slid outside with Trevarow.

"Where would she go?" Trevarow asked.

"Head for Bridgeport, is my guess," Spur said. "She might stop and bury the gold somewhere first, then try to get lost in Bridgeport or on toward Sacramento."

"Be damn handy to have a telegraph about now," Trevarow said.

"She won't ride a horse, a buggy maybe. Does the mine have a stable, any rigs? Wagons?"

John led Spur on a short run across the mine area to a small stable built in back of a storage shed. A bearded man was just about to blow out a lantern.

"Damn, Sheriff. More people out and about tonight."

"Mrs. Bechtel. Did she just have you hitch up a buggy for her?"

"Yeah, how'd you know?"

"Was Eli Johl with her?"

"True. Said they had to drive to Aurora fast to be there for an important meeting tomorrow. Something about buying another mine."

"Anybody else going with her? Any riders for protection?"

The bearded man scratched his head under a bill cap. "Dad blamed but you sure know a lot. Yeah. She asked me to try to get two men from the mill to ride along with them. But I couldn't find anybody who would do it, not even for ten dollars. They left about five minutes ago."

"Thanks," Spur said.

Both men ran for the horses that Spur said were close by. They had seen Deputy Jones head over to the doctor's office.

"We can stop by at the jail for hand guns," Trevarow said. "You still have that Spencer?"

"In the boot," Spur said. "Then we head out south."

"What if they go north?"

"Not a chance."

A half hour later Spur knelt in the trail that led out of Bodie to the south and west and found recent buggy tracks.

"We're on the right track!" Spur shouted and they stepped into their stirrups and rode.

"They in a one-horse buggy?" Trevarow asked.

"Looks like it. One horse for damn sure, making good time along here, but that can't last long."

Spur and Trevarow galloped for a quarter of a mile, then let the horses slow down to a walk for a mile before Spur lifted his mount into a canter.

"Eat up five to six miles an hour this way with most horses," Spur said. "That buggy be good if it can average three miles an hour."

"Eli Johl is wounded, that might hold them up a bit. He could bleed to death if he doesn't wrap up that shoulder."

They rode hard for a half hour, then stopped and listened. They couldn't hear anything ahead. Spur took some dry grass, lit it with a stinker match and checked the trail ahead of their horses' prints.

"We still have a hot trail here. Can't be too much farther ahead of us."

Again they rode. They topped a small rise and Spur motioned for them to stop. This time they could hear the jangle of harness and the creaking of a going-dry wheel hub.

Both riders kicked their mounts into a gallop and shortly they saw the buggy in the misty darkness ahead of them. Spur put a pistol shot over the top of the rig, but the driver urged the horse to pull the buggy faster.

"Remember, they've both got guns!" Trevarow shouted.

Spur nodded, pulled the Spencer from his scabbard and sent a .52 caliber round through the top of the buggy. It didn't slow the rig a bit.

A pistol cracked from the back of the buggy, then again. Spur and Trevarow slowed and hung back out of range.

"I'll get in front of them," Spur said. "The trail takes a long circle route here. I can cut across and beat them, then stop them from in front."

161

"I want them both alive," Trevarow said.

"So do I. I'll think of something. You keep firing now and then to let them know we're still here."

Spur cut into the open country next to the trail. All he had to worry about were gophers or squirrel holes. He charged the horse across the dry, barren hill away from the stage road, then turned when he was lost in the darkness and cut back toward the trail ahead.

It wasn't much of a long arc, but Spur figured it would be enough with his better speed. When he came back to the stage road he saw the first few spindly trees along the route. He rode ahead into a small grove and jumped down, searching the ground. He found what he was hunting, a four-inch thick tree that had died and fallen over years ago. It had branches and was about twenty feet long.

Quickly Spur grabbed it and tugged it free of the ground and grasses, then ran with it into the trail so it lay across the stage coach road.

When the horse saw it, the animal might stop, try to go around it or plow into it and stumble. It was the best chance Spur had to stop the buggy without shooting the horse.

He tied his mount to a bush and lifted out the Spencer, levering a new round into the breech.

The harness jangled in front of him and in only a few seconds the buggy came charging down the trail toward the small roadblock. With good luck the horse might not shy and charge straight across. The buggy would bounce mightily, but could get over the roadblock. It was possible.

Almost too late the horse saw the obstruction. She shied to one side. The driver tried to pull her back, then the animal was into the small branches.

The mare felt the limbs on her legs and stopped suddenly. The traces creaked and the single-tree rattled. The light buggy bumped her forward two feet, but the horse refused to draw the buggy a bit farther.

"Ease out of there with your hands up!" Spur barked. He shot over the buggy with his pistol for emphasis, then jumped two feet to the side in case there was return fire.

Only silence came from the buggy.

"I said, get down from there, or I'm going to start shooting inside the rig!"

This time a figure stepped out. A man. His hands were in the air.

"Don't shoot, I don't have the gun."

"Lay down on the trail, now!" Spur bellowed.

The man lay down.

"Mrs. Bechtel, you might as well come out. The chase is over. You've lost."

Three shots thundered from the blackness of the buggy. One slapped through an inch of Spur's left arm. He spun around and fired twice into the buggy. Then he ran forward, made it to the back of the buggy and moved quickly around it.

Trevarow rode up.

"She's gone," Spur said. "She just took three shots at me and must have ran into the brush over there." Spur sent two rounds from his pistol into the small brush and smattering of trees to the right of the buggy.

Spur glared into the darkness. "John, you take care of things here. Check to see if the gold is still there, and then tie up Johl. I'm going to get this hellcat and bring her back for trial. Oh, first, could you tie my bandana around my arm. She nicked me with a shot.''

Trevarow put a pressure pad under the bandage to help stop the blood, then tied it tightly.

"You're going to try to find her in the dark?"

"If she moves I'll know it. If not I'll find her when it gets light. Can't be more than three hours now until daylight."

Spur looked at the darkness of the woods, and without another word charged twenty feet into the thin trees and brush. Once inside the light growth, he stopped and listened. He heard nothing.

There was no rush, he had the rest of the night and then all morning. If she ran, she wouldn't get far. He still carried the rifle and his Colt.

Ahead maybe twenty yards he heard a branch snap, then another. Spur fired toward the spot but high so he would not wound Milly Bechtel.

A scream of fury answered his shots. Spur moved ahead gently, not breaking a twig, stepping down only when he was sure that it would not make any noise. He moved ten yards before he heard more noise.

It came from straight ahead. The leaves on the light brush killed any attempt the moon made to break through with some faint light. It was as dark as a coal mine.

Spur moved ahead again, and this time the sounds came from his right. The growth followed a small water course, which probably was wet only after a good soaking rain. He stepped that way cautiously.

Two shots blasted from the direction ahead, but the rounds went well behind him. Spur did not return the fire. He walked faster now. They were working uphill. The gentle little valley and the growth would peter out soon.

Spur heard sounds again, up hill. He ran ten yards toward the spot, making no attempt to be quiet, then dove to the ground. A pair of shots blazed in the darkness. They came from directly ahead not fifteen feet.

"If you're the one back there, McCoy, you're a dead son of a bitch. I know how to use these .45's I have. I used to practice twenty rounds a day with one I own. Come on and get me, McCoy."

As she spoke he used the sound of her voice to cover his movements as he worked another five feet forward.

Then she ran to the side. He heard the sounds. She was moving out of the brush! It didn't make sense. Why? He moved silently to the edge of the growth in time to see Milly Bechtel fade into the darkness of the barren, rocky soil covered slope that extended upward.

A few clouds that had been flirting with the moon swept away and he saw her standing in a formal dueling pose, sideways, pistol up and ready. He stepped into the moonlight then dodged to one side and back into the darkness of the brush as she fired.

Spur dropped to the ground and rolled to the side.

Milly laughed. "I told you I could use this weapon."

"Sure, but how many rounds do you have left? Did you bring a spare box of .44 rounds with you, or are they still in your reticule back in the buggy?"

"Oh, damn!"

"It's a long walk to Bridgeport, Milly. Why not give it up? You'll get a fair trial."

Spur rolled deeper into the darkness and Milly fired twice again. The rounds came seriously close to where he had been speaking.

Spur thought it through. He could stumble around out there on the side of the hill looking for her. The chances of finding her waiting for him with two cocked .44's was too great.

He could sit here and wait, watching until dawn, then take the rifle and go out and track her down. She wouldn't go far in the darkness. Even if she did she would be worn out by dawn and he could find her quickly.

He chose the wait method and settled down. Twice he heard shots in the distance. They came from up the slope somewhere, so she was moving. She must have thought she heard him coming up below her.

Spur dozed once. A squirrel ran through the brush and he came awake with his six-gun. He heard the animal again and tried to stay awake.

Just at dawn he moved to the very edge of the growth and looked out. The ridge sloped up a quarter of a mile. It was as barren as most of the rest of the timberless slopes around Bodie. A splotch of sage here and there, a few weeds, a wild flower or two and that was it. Nothing a person could hide behind.

He rubbed his eyes, reloaded his six-gun and moved out at a brisk walk up the slope. He found her tracks almost at once. There seemed to be no try at hiding the direction of travel. She had continued up the slope about halfway, then doubled back toward the stage road again.

She would wait for the first stage or wagon to come along heading for Bridgeport and ask for a lift. Spur moved faster then, found where her prints entered the brushy section again and now walked with more care. He checked the landscape ahead, watched for places she might be hiding.

Twenty minutes later he came back to the stage road. In a powdery dusty part of the trail he checked it carefully. There were insect trails and mice tracks over the stage coach and wagon tracks. The bugs came out at night, so the tracks had not been made early this morning. No wagon or stage had been past here going either direction.

So where was Milly Bechtel?

Her tracks stuck to the road a ways, then vanished into some small brush along the side. It led nowhere. Spur jogged to the end of the small trees and found her tracks on the stage trail again.

He jogged forward, the rifle in one hand, his six-gun in the other. He topped a small rise and started down a mile long hill. Milly sat at the edge of the road two hundred yards ahead. She seemed to be rocking back and forth.

Spur sent a shot over her head with the rifle. She didn't seem to notice. He put another shot that dug up dirt in the road five feet in front of her, but the woman didn't move.

McCoy walked toward her slowly, his six-gun ready. At a hundred yards he could see little, but at fifty, he could tell she sat in the dust of the trail, her arms were folded and she rocked forward and back, forward and back. Milly faced him and she appeared to have neither of the weapons she had the night before.

Spur moved up cautiously. Unless the guns were under her skirts somewhere, she didn't have them.

"Milly, are you all right?"

She didn't reply.

"Milly, I've come to take you home with me, are you ready to go?"

Again, no response. Spur heard something behind him and looked over his shoulder to see a buggy coming. Two horses trailed it on leads and he saw John Trevarow driving.

Spur put the rifle down and touched her shoulder with his hand. "Milly?"

There was no response. She looked straight ahead and now he could hear a little tune she was singing. Something about "Now I lay me down to sleep . . . ." It was a child's prayer at bedtime.

The buggy stopped a few yards away. Spur motioned Trevarow to come and see her.

"Mrs. Bechtel, it's time to go back to Bodie now," John said.

There was no response.

Spur holstered his pistol, saw John draw his. Spur knelt in the dust beside her, took her hand and lifted her. She stood with no more urging. Spur felt a little self conscious doing it, but he patted down her skirt to be sure there was no pistol hidden in it. Then he led her to the buggy and she sat in the seat but continued to stare straight ahead.

Eli Johl looked at her and snorted. "Crazy as a loon. I had a cousin that did that. Never said a word again as long as she lived. Her mind just snapped." Johl looked away, then turned to McCoy. "This robbery was all her idea, the gold robbery. She said we could get rich and sell the mine and go live in St. Louis or maybe Chicago."

Captain Trevarow brought up Spur's horse.

"Mr. Johl here has agreed to turn state's evidence against Mrs. Bechtel if we let him testify for the prosecution," Trevarow said. "He explained to me in detail how they robbed the first Wells Fargo stage. One of the men's mask slipped and a guard recognized him the way we figured. After the robbery they melted down the Standard bullion and recast it in Bechtel bullion molds."

"Did you agree to get him a light sentence?" Spur asked.

"No. We talked about it. But now with Mrs. Bechtel beyond prosecution, I don't see why we should let Eli off for the ten men he killed or caused to have killed."

Spur smiled. "Good, I might even stay around to watch the hanging. Now, let's get this thing turned around and head back to Bodie. We've got gold here to return to Standard, and a bunch of law man kind of things to get done."

10

The first project Spur and Captain Trevarow did involved convincing Doc Rogers that he should hold Milly Bechtel in the one small patient room he had at his medical office.

"Doc, you can watch her and deal with any medical problems that we never could in jail. I'll put through the formal charges but she needs to be taken to the state Insane Asylum. She's crazier than a hooty owl."

As they talked Milly sat on a chair in the office looking straight ahead. She responded only to touch and motions. Spur was not sure if she could hear or if she understood the words.

Doc washed out the bullet hole on Spur's left arm.

"Lucky, son, the slug missed the bone. Gets nasty when a round smashes an arm bone. Put you out of business for six months at least. Now this kind of thing I can deal with. With them mental problems, the crazies, I just don't know what in hell to do for them."

"Doc, all you have to do is keep her in that room with a bolt on the outside. County'll even buy the damned bolt and put it on. Come on, Doc, I got no facilities to take care of a woman over at the jail."

"So you think I do? Somebody's got to feed her, change her clothes, clean up after her. Maybe even watch she don't kill herself. How long would it be?"

"A week, Doc, maybe two. You figure out the cost and the county will pay for her keep."

"Not a boarding house I got here, John." He finished bandaging Spur's arm and relented. "All right, she can stay. Maybe she'll snap out of it."

Captain Trevarow took the 75 pounds of gold bars back to the Standard Mining Company. They told Dan Cook that the Bechtel had melted the bullion and recast them into Bechtel imprints. He should do the same thing turning them into Standard again. He was surprised and pleased. He gave Captain Trevarow a receipt for the 75 pounds of gold which he would turn over to the Wells Fargo company.

They stowed the buggy back at the Bechtel mine. Production had stopped. There didn't seem to be anyone to take over. Sheriff's Captain Trevarow appointed two men from the Standard as temporary administrators of the company until the legal entanglements could be worked out. They had operational powers only.

Dan Cook and a man from the Bodie mine met with the men and arranged an overview committee to keep tabs on the functioning of the mine until some legal arrangements could be made. Whoever now owned the mine, the Bechtel heirs or estate, would be well protected.

Spur filled out the final report at the sheriff's

office and then headed for his hotel and a good long sleep.

Captain Trevarow was pleased with the way the whole operation had turned out. They had nailed down the gold robbers and killers. He was still questioning Eli Johl in his cell to get the names of the first band of robbers who had shot down the guards. He had two of them, including Lenny whom they had found dead. That left four more. He would get the names and put out wanted notices on them all.

Trevarow left the jail for a walk over to the Chop House for his usual midday bowl of soup and cup of coffee.

Ahead on the boardwalk two miners were snarling at each other. The insults turned into name calling as Trevarow approached.

"You're nothing but a thieving mine rat!" one man shouted.

"Mine rat, am I?" the other screamed. "How would you know when you live at the bottom of the outhouse pit!"

People began moving away from the pair. Both had six-guns on their hips.

Trevarow walked up as the man's hands hovered over their weapons. They stood ten feet apart. Somebody was going to be killed.

Trevarow jumped between the men, holding his hands out palms out, fingers up in a stop motion.

"Hold it, you two jackasses!" Trevarow bellowed. "If there's any killing gonna be done in my town, then I'm gonna do it. Gunplay in Bodie is illegal. You fire that weapon and you spend thirty days in jail whether you hit anybody or not. You wound somebody you get six months at hard labor, most likely wood splitting. You want that?

"Let's say you get lucky and actually kill somebody. Why then you're gonna hang. No questions. No self defense garbage. You kill somebody in Bodie, I'm gonna get you hung. Had enough of this damn foolishness."

The men's hands eased away from iron.

"Haven't I seen you two drinking together? I thought you were friends."

"Friends? With that bastard?"

The other man snorted. "Aw, hell, I won't spark her no more. You can have her. I'll find me another girl. Just . . . just don't say I never done nothing for you."

"Hell, Will, guess I got a little het up at you. But I saw her first. Ain't that many pretty gals left in Bodie."

The two men stared at each other a minute.

"Hell, Will, let me buy you a beer. Maybe she's got a sister."

The two men walked away talking about the nice girls in town, and wondering who to take to the dance coming up at the Union Hall on Saturday night.

Will motioned to the crowd.

"All right, the excitement's all over. Move along here. Don't clog up the boardwalk. People have business to do along here without wanting to walk in the street."

Spur had walked back to his room at the U.S. Hotel. As soon as he stepped inside, he glanced around quickly. Nothing had been changed or moved. He locked the door, pushed a straight back chair under it and fell on the bed. As he did he felt something. When he picked it up it was a piece of paper.

"McCoy. I figured you'd be home sometime last night. You never did come. I got free and come down for a nice quiet evening with you. Maybe later." It was signed Jessica.

Spur grinned, pulled off his boots and his shirt, then dropped on the hard bed and was sleeping almost at once. He didn't even have time to think about food.

After the sheriff had his soup and coffee, he lit up a short black cigar. It had been a good day so far: the murders and gold robbery solved and a put down of a shootout on the street.

For the first time he realized that he had talked the gunnies out of shooting and he wasn't even wearing his own .45. Yes, he had done it. He didn't *need* his six-gun. He could take care of a lot of the small problems around town just by talking it out with the people involved.

Back on the street, he walked the town. He hadn't done that for a month or two. The jeweler came running out of his store when he saw Trevarow.

"Captain! Look at this. Somebody gave me a counterfeit twenty dollar gold piece. I always check the gold, but somehow this one slipped through."

"Could I see it?" Trevarow asked.

The merchant held it out and the lawman took it. He could see it was a poor imitation. "I have an expert on counterfeiting from Washington who's in town. I'm sure he'll want to see this poor imitation."

"But . . . but what about my twenty dollars?"

"The coin is worthless. Maybe fifteen or twenty cents worth of gold over the lead."

"But I can give it to someone else."

"Then I'd have to arrest you for passing a counterfeit coin. I'll take care of it. Sorry, it's your loss. Be more careful of the coins you accept."

"Yes sir," the jeweler said and went back in his shop.

Trevarow shook his head. Anyone stupid enough to take that spurious a gold coin as genuine, deserved to lose the twenty dollars. He almost relented. The twenty dollars was probably all the profit the man made all week.

Down the street a shot blasted into the usual noises and the clanking of the stamp mills. Trevarow hurried in that direction. He found a man standing over another, a six-gun in his hand. The man on the ground had a wound to his chest.

"Somebody go get Doc Rogers!" Trevarow shouted. "You!" he said, pointing to a man standing nearby. The man turned and ran to the doctor's office.

Trevarow ignored the gun in the man's hand, pushed him aside and checked the victim. He was still breathing. The bullet had missed his heart but probably hit a lung.

Trevarow stood slowly. The shooter still held the gun. "This man was unarmed," the law man said.

"He called me a liar!" the gunman shouted. "Nobody calls Marvin Anderson a liar and gets away with it."

"Are you a liar?" Trevarow asked.

The gunman looked up quickly just in time to see Trevarow's right fist crash into his jaw and the lawman's left hand grab his right wrist in a vice and shake the gun to the dust. Trevarow spun the man around, forcing his right hand upward behind his back.

A Deputy Sheriff ran up then, and the Captain pushed the gunman toward him.

"Lock him up," Trevarow said. "We'll see if we charge him with murder or attempted murder."

Doc Rogers came a few minutes later, panting and out of breath. He knelt on the boardwalk beside the wounded man and scowled.

"Still alive, but he's unconscious. Get a door so we can take him over to my office. That bullet has to come out or he won't have a chance to live."

Trevarow ran into the hardware store and came back with an unpainted door. They put the victim on it and four men carried it toward Doc's office.

"Let me know what happens, Rogers," Captain Trevarow said. He waved the people away and they went about their business.

He turned in at a saloon, the Gold Digger, and asked for a beer. The barkeep drew him a mug full from a keg and grinned. "On the house, Sheriff. I like to have you drop in now and then. It tends to quiet down any unruly customers I have. And the poker games suddenly become as honest as rummy games in a preacher's parlor."

The captain nodded his thanks, but tossed a dime on the counter anyway. "I'll be around, time to time, but I pay my way and I expect my deputies to pay also. I don't want to hear about you trying to bribe my men with free drinks."

"No sir, Captain Trevarow, I wouldn't do that. I like it better that way."

"Good. Things are going to start shaping up around this town or I'm gonna be knocking heads. You can help spread the word that gun play and wild sprees are over in Bodie."

Trevarow finished his beer, waved at the men in the saloon and walked out the door.

The barkeep wiped sweat off his forehead when the lawmen had left. "Damn but that man is tough! I saw how he stopped that gunfight up the street. You can tell everyone that John Trevarow might have hung up his six-gun but he's still as tough as hell. Just don't mess with Sheriff Captain Trevarow or you're looking for more trouble than you can handle."

Some of the men at the bar lifted their mugs of beer in agreement.

Spur McCoy had slept until late afternoon, then went into the dining room for the biggest dinner on the menu. It had just come and he was starting to eat, when a young man no more than twenty-five walked in and stared at him.

A moment later the man came over to Spur's table and stood three feet back. Spur saw him and knew in a second what he was. Gunman. There was no mistaking the pose, the tied down leather holster, the hogleg hanging loose, ready and the gunhand that hovered over the butt of the weapon.

"I'm looking for Spur McCoy," the young man said.

"You found him," Spur answered but went on eating as if the man wasn't there.

"I hear Billy Deadman died yesterday."

"True."

"How did he die?"

"He ate his own .45 muzzle and put a slug through the top of his head."

"Liar! Billy would never do that."

"If you knew him so well, where were you when he needed you?"

"I . . . I was busy."

"Did you go examine his body closely and see the three sets of rattlesnake fang marks on his left arm?"

"Liar!"

"Sonny, that's the second time you've said that.

If I was the type to get upset easily, I'd have to teach you not to throw around dangerous accusations that way. You have a chance to withdraw the words."

"Not a chance. I know Billy. He was fast. You could never beat him. He'd never kill himself."

"You ever been bitten by a rattlesnake, boy?"

"No. And I ain't no boy. My name is Dorsey."

"Well, Mr. Dorsey, if you've never been bit once, let alone three times on the same arm, how do you know what you would do and wouldn't do when the burning, searing, unbearable pain started to gush through your bloodstream like liquid fire?"

"Didn't come here to jawbone you, McCoy. Last thing Billy said to me was he had a skunk to kill and he'd be right back, half hour at the most."

"Said that, did he? I called him out for a showdown outside of town and he brought a rifle and started shooting from fifty yards. Killed my horse first thing. A real sportsman, your friend Billy. Is that how he built his reputation?"

Dorsey's face got red, he couldn't speak for a minute, then he sputtered. "Damn you! He never did no such thing. He could beat you fair and square!"

"Like the night he threw a bomb in my hotel room. That was fair and square? Your hero was a sidewinder who killed however he could, maybe even face to face. But I couldn't swear he did it honest, cause I've never seen him try that."

"Outside, McCoy! Right now! I'd gun you down in here but it might upset the people's dinner. Out!" He drew his six-gun and Spur knew he was fast. He held the gun leveled at Spur as they stared at each other.

Spur stood slowly, kept his hand away from his

pistol and went into the lobby.

"How about the alley, then your wild shots won't kill anybody."

"My only shot will be in your heart, McCoy."

They walked to the alley, Spur ahead. He had no fears that this kid would shoot him in the back. The young man wanted to prove that he was faster, better.

In the alley, Spur stopped and turned around. Dorsey stood thirty-five feet away.

"You ready, big gunman with a bigger mouth?" Dorsey asked.

"Whenever you are."

They stood facing each other. A woman came out of a store down from the hotel, then hurried back inside. Two men stood at the end of the alley, then scurried back to the street and safety.

Spur watched Dorsey, his eyes would give away his move.

There had been no conscious thought in Spur McCoy's head that Dorsey was drawing his six-gun. Suddenly Spur's hand flew up his side, the gun butt slammed in his hand and his left palm stroked back the hammer to full cock. Then the weapon continued to rise and fired in a blinding fast move that was mirrored on the other end. Both rounds went off at almost the same time making one booming roar in the alley.

Spur felt the bullet hit his side. It slammed him halfway around. He kept his weapon trained on Dorsey who looked at McCoy with wide eyes, then he staggered backwards with the force of Spur's .45 slug and fell to one side, his weapon skidding away from his hand.

Spur walked forward slowly. His left hand covered a red spot on his left side where blood oozed through his shirt. Dorsey lay crumpled on his back and his side. Somebody ran out of the hotel and rolled Dorsey over on his back.

"Damn, right through the heart!" the man said. "He was dead before he hit the dirt! What a shot, and from thirty-five maybe forty feet!"

Spur looked at the man. "Call the Sheriff's Captain. Tell him I'll be over to Doc Roger's place when he wants to talk."

Trevarow found Spur there twenty minutes later. He had taken statements from three witnesses in the dining room, and the one man at the scene.

"Another inch to the right and you would have been in deep trouble, young man," Doc Rogers said. "Just missed your kidney and your bowel. Went clean through. That's two more bullet holes in your hide. How many does that make now?"

"A few, Doc. Now hush up, the law is here to arrest me for holding a gunfight in the city limits."

Trevarow snorted. "You were damn lucky, McCoy. That boy was fast. Probably a good thing you didn't know the rest of his name."

"More than Dorsey?"

"Yeah, Little Boy Dorsey."

McCoy whistled. "The kid who gunned down three Texas Rangers and took out that bank? The one who is getting called an executioner because he plain likes to kill people?"

"The same one. He was the only one recognized on that bank job. Chances are that Billy Deadman was one of the other three men. Deadman always did travel with a pack."

"Dorsey was fast. If he'd been a little more accurate, we both would be dead right now."

"Seen it happen, but only once." Trevarow snorted. "Damn sure it wasn't around Bodie. Most of these miners and wood men in town couldn't hit the floor they were standing on with three shots."

"I guess I'll live, Sheriff. How much is my fine?"

"No fine, I'm running you out of town—in a week or so when you start to heal up. Oh, Johnson, the Wells Fargo guy wants to see us, something important. You feel like taking a walk or you want a horse, maybe a buggy?"

"I'm ready. Doc, how is Milly?"

"About the same. She won't eat, but she'll take food when we feed her. Strange damn thing. Like she just turned off a switch and won't live normal but don't want to die."

The two men said goodbye to Doc Rogers and walked up to the Wells Fargo office. It was almost six o'clock by then. Johnson waved them into his office.

A tall slender man wearing all black sat in Johnson's usual chair behind his desk. There were some reports spread out in front of him. He looked up and then stood.

Johnson made the introductions. The new man's name was Jacob Linden, vice president in charge of security of Wells Fargo.

"I'm from the San Francisco office. Wanted to come out and see if we could get to the bottom of this robbery. The company doesn't like to lose twenty-five thousand dollars on a secured shipment. Gives other robbers ideas."

"Mr. Linden, I'd say the man most responsible for the recovery of the gold was Mr. McCoy, here," Johnson said.

"What's this all about?" Spur asked.

"Why, the reward, of course," Linden said. "Now that the gold has been recovered and we've had a release from our guarantee by Standard Mining

Company, we are more than pleased to present the reward to the one most responsible for the recovery of the gold.''

"That's good of you, Mr. Linden, but I'm not the right person. I'm a federal law officer and not allowed to accept rewards. The person who gave us the key to the whole case was Jessica Wright.''

Captain Trevarow looked up at Spur with surprise.

Then the Captain nodded. "Yes, she was the one who angled us onto Eli Johl, and the Bechtel. Without her lead we wouldn't have the slightest idea who did it.''

"Well, then, I'll make out a bank draft in her name for the amount of five percent of the recovery, that's one thousand, two hundred and fifty dollars. What was that name again?''

Spur told him.

"Why don't I go bring Miss Wright down here to the office so Mr. Linden can present the bank draft to her?'' Spur asked. "I'm sure that he'll want to thank her in person as well.''

"Yes, yes, that's a good idea, McCoy. Now that this is all cleared up, I'll want to do an inspection of all our facilities here tomorrow, then take the stage out.''

"I won't be more than an hour. Why don't we meet right here,'' Spur said.

They nodded and Spur walked out of the Wells Fargo office and headed for Virgin Alley. When he told Jessica about her sudden wealth, she thought he was joking.

"Big companies like Wells Fargo don't give whores like me no reward,'' Jessica said.

He caught her by her shoulders. "Jessica Wright, that's what I told him your name was because I didn't know your other one. I didn't see any reason to tell him about your current occupation. That is, your ex-profession. As of now you're the widow Wright heading for San Diego to open that boarding house!''

She threw her arms around his neck and kissed him. Then her eyes widened. "Oh, glory! I got to get fancied up in some proper clothes. Do I have any? That one dress might do. And I got to do my hair and take off most of my face paint . . .''

"You have an hour," Spur told her.

"I'll need two days!''

They made it is just under an hour. Mr. Linden was properly impressed by the demure widow, Jessica Wright. Captain Trevarow hardly recognized her, and Johnson had never seen her before. The little ceremony went off nicely.

"I'd think it would be best not to let this get in the newspapers," Spur said. "The whole story of the recovery is fine, but the news about the reward might just make somebody want to steal gold and then be the one to 'find' and return it.''

Linden agreed with Spur and no word was to leak out to anyone outside of the room.

Twenty minutes later, Spur and Jessica slipped up the back stairs at the U.S. Hotel and walked into Spur's room.

"I never did get to finish my supper. You stay right here and I'll go down to the dining room and have them send up a great dinner for two. Don't tell me what you want. You rich women will have to get used to being waited on.''

He came back a few minutes later and their dinner followed in another twenty minutes. They had roast beef, oysters and trout to start, together with four kinds of vegetables in cheese sauce and three deserts. There were two kinds of wine.

"Mercy, I'll be fat as a poland china hog," Jessica said.

"Not a chance. First we eat, and then we get some exercise and work off all of the fat."

"What kind of exercise?"

"We'll think of something."

She grinned, then sobered. "You really think I could make a go of it in San Diego?"

"Damn right! The town is growing, going to be a real city one of these years. Nice little seaport there, and plenty of sun and open spaces. Not much rain, but eventually they'll figure out how to bring in water. Why not give it a try?"

It took them nearly an hour to do justice to all the food. Spur couldn't remember when he'd eaten so much. Everything was well cooked and the foods were all his favorites.

When they were through with the big tray, he sat all the leavings in the hall, and locked the door.

Jessica patted the bed beside her and he sat down. She reached over and kissed his lips gently.

"How . . ." tears filled her eyes. "How can I ever thank you, Spur McCoy, for . . . for the other time, and now this. I've never even heard of that much money!" She took the bank draft out of her reticule and stared at it.

"Sometimes I can make twenty dollars a week, but I never get to keep it all, and even so . . . I bet I couldn't save a thousand dollars in five years!"

"So, by telling the sheriff about what you heard, you just saved five years out of your young life."

She blinked, and then blew her nose. "I still . . . I still can't believe it. I told Hetti. She said Godspeed.

She's been more a mother to me than my real mother.''

Spur kissed the tears off her cheeks.

"Couldn't have happened to a nicer lady."

"This widow Wright. What if somebody asks me to see my marriage license and my husband's death certificate?''

"Nobody will. Most folks can't prove that they're married. Out here in the west it isn't where you come from or who you are, it's how you act and what you do. You act respectable, and everyone will believe you're who you say you are."

"Come with me, McCoy! Help me get established in San Diego and stay a month or so."

"Hey, I've got a job to do. A boss to report to. Which I better think about doing. I'm glad there's no telegraph here. Where is the closest one . . . Sacramento, probably. Maybe Carson City.''

"You're wounded! You can't go back to work for days yet!''

"Maybe I could squeeze out two or three days to recuperate. That is if I had good nursing.''

"You've got the best nurse in all of Bodie!''

"Good, Doc Rogers will be pleased.''

She fiddled with the little jacket that went over the top of her dress.

"Spur, do I still have to act respectable? I mean, in here with you?''

"What did you have in mind?''

"Well, since I'm a widow and all, I was thinking I might test you out for husband material. Test you in the only way that most women think is practical.''

"In bed?''

"Exactly.''

"Mrs. Wright, I don't think it would be unseemly of you to do that. What married folks, and unmarried folks do behind the closed door of their bedroom is nobody's business."

"Mr. McCoy, I like the way you put things."

She slid out of the jacket and stood and quickly whipped the dress over her head. Then she sat on the bed in her tight white drawers and the chemise that couldn't quite conceal her pink tipped breasts.

"Mr. McCoy, I'd like to give you a test. First you have to kiss me about twenty times—just anywhere that you want to. Then if you pass that test, we'll move on to some others that I have in mind."

She grinned at him.

"Mr. McCoy, I'm starting the test right now."

Three days later they left Bodie on the stage and headed out to Bridgeport, then retraced part of their route to get to Sacramento.

Jessica still had the Wells Fargo bank draft safely hidden in her reticule. She had saved almost two hundred dollars and that would be plenty to get her all the way to San Diego.

They registered in the California Hotel as Mr. and Mrs. Charles Wright, and Spur left her there and found the telegraph office. The wire he sent was clear and concise.

CAPITOL INVESTIGATIONS
WASHINGTON, D.C.
GENERAL WILTON D. HALLECK

IN SACRAMENTO. MUST GO TO SAN FRANCISCO ON URGENT PERSONAL BUSINESS. CONTACT ME THERE AT PACIFIC HOTEL WITH ANY NEW ASSIGNMENT. LEFT BODIE, CAL. TWO DAYS AGO AFTER SOLVING EIGHT

MURDERS IN A GOLD ROBBERY. U.S.
MINT GOLD INVOLVED, SO I BECAME
INVOLVED. READY FOR DUTY TWO
DAYS HENCE.

When he got back to the hotel, he found that
"Mrs. Wright" had visited three shops in Sacramento to fill out her wardrobe. The clothes were respectable, well made, and well within her budget.

"I must have something to wear on the boat to
San Diego. You did say the boat would be the best
way to go."

Spur laughed and agreed with her, then took her
out to dinner.

That night as they lay in the bed, Spur McCoy
thought ahead to San Francisco. It had been a year
or more since he'd been there. He wondered how it
had changed. It was a dynamic city. He tried to remember the last problem he had heard about there.
He'd been in New Mexico at the time.

Perhaps Fleurette Leon in his St. Louis office
would have something ready for him to tackle once
he got to San Francisco. He hoped she would.

"Hey, you were a thousand miles away," Jessica
said.

She rolled over on top of him and he realized she
had taken off the nightgown. She rubbed against
him, bent to kiss his lips and grinned. "Hey, I have
you for only another two days. I'm going to do my
best to wear you right down to a nub before I'm
through with you."

Spur laughed. "That's a challenge that I don't
want to pass up," he said and reached up and kissed
her lips.